TRUMPERY

VIRGINIA DALE

NEWMAN SPRINGS PUBLISHING
320 Broad Street
Red Bank, NJ 07701

First originally published by Newman Springs Publishing 2022

Cover art by Virginia Dale

ISBN 978-1-63881-931-8 (Paperback)
ISBN 978-1-63881-932-5 (Digital)

Printed in the United States of America

To Freda Mae Davis

Chapter 1

West Virginia parted ways with the state of Virginia in 1861 due to its refusal to fight for the Confederacy. Most of the people voted against slavery and to stay with the Union although many slave owners voted to join the Confederacy. After the Union won the Civil War, more than a few formed Ku Klux Klan chapters, copying former slave holders in the southern states. Since West Virginia depended largely upon coal mining for its livelihood, workers' rights were well regarded by the majority of its citizens.

When the newly elected senator Bill Jameson, a descendant of former plantation owners, shook hands with the older senator whose seat he had just won by a narrow margin, he was surprised to see tears in the older politician's eyes. Since when was it acceptable for a former senator to make such an unseemly display of emotion?

They stood silhouetted by the stately domed Capitol in Washington, D.C. As the television cameras pointed at them, Morrow wished him well and said that the well-being of the workers in this coal mining state depended on him.

Jameson scowled at his defeated opponent, noting that he was wearing an off-the-rack suit and laughed in his face. "Of course, they'll be well taken care of. Why do you think they voted for me?"

Morrow, the older senator, shook his head in confusion. He couldn't understand why the people had voted for a man better known for his success on Wall Street than for his concern for the ordinary working class that he, Morrow, had fought for with a large degree of success for over thirty years. Not to mention the voting rights he and Congressman John Lewis had fought hard for in their separate states; they'd rallied each other when there was opposition. Something had changed in the past year. He had seen many of his

5

former colleagues in the US Senate defeated by much younger men with no experience in protecting anyone's rights other than perhaps their own.

"Will you continue to fight for clean coal mining? For clean air and streams?" he asked, his brow furrowed with anger. His shock of thick white hair shone in the sunlight.

Jameson tried to keep a straight face, but he couldn't help laughing. "I'll fight for the almighty dollar to enrich this state," he replied with a hearty laugh issuing from his handsome face that had a distinctive furrow between his brows.

"You'll find a stiff opposition," said Morrow, clenching and unclenching his fists.

Bill Jameson's election to the US Senate at the age of thirty-five astounded many of the constituents of his poverty-stricken state. That they would reject the salt-of-the-earth senator whose hair was now white, his face creased but not wrinkled and still unbowed with a strength that came from having worked in the shafts of coal mines himself, was unconscionable, but people can be swayed by youth and glib talk.

Feeling her husband push her forward, Jameson's lovely Russian-born wife stepped forward and declared, "My husband knows how to make things work. We're all going to get rich."

She tossed her elegant blond hair so that it framed her face to perfection. She smiled even though she was furious at him for pushing her; but she, better than anyone, knew the repercussions if she didn't do what he wanted her to. She, too, held back tears as she thought of her late husband and of her fifteen-year-old daughter, whom she'd left with her sister when she'd had to flee Russia because she'd asked too many questions about her late husband's untimely death. When a grenade was tossed into her living room, she had left that same day, her sister assuring her that her daughter, Nadia, would be well cared for. She'd married this wealthy American with the hope of finding safety and even love. He gave her another unsubtle push forward. She almost screamed. She hadn't found love with Jameson.

That's what I get for marrying a goy, she thought, breathing heavily, feeling like crying as her thoughts flashed to her loving Russian husband and their daughter, Nadia.

They were always on her mind. She'd married Jameson hoping he could help her daughter get out of Russia.

Morrow stepped forward and waited to speak again. His coat was rumpled. He lacked the expensive Armani suit and the cocksure youth of Jameson.

He felt such pain that he said, "Making things work means passing legislation to help our hard-pressed people. That takes dedication. You must constantly be on your guard for laws that would undermine our efforts. You can't run a state like a business. You have to roll your sleeves up and truck with our common folk, and you have to love them. You are young and stylishly dressed, but will you work for people down on their luck?"

Memories of the famous coal miners' strike in 1913 when Black and white miners had fought side by side for more humane conditions made Morrow wince. The miners always referred back to it when things got bad. Things always got bad in the mines.

He and Jameson faced off. Jameson felt his face reddening. How dare this inferior criticize his intentions?

"Look, Mr. Morrow, the campaign is over. I'm tired of hearing about clean this and clean that. I intend to clean house!"

Morrow clenched his fists. Blood surged to his temples. He had never met such a brash, self-seeking individual. "I fear the voters have made a terrible mistake, Senator Jameson. I hope I'm wrong because I love this country."

He wiped his nose on his coat sleeve and looked out at the crowd in front of him. He didn't recognize a soul. These people were not the old-timers, but slickly dressed, very young newcomers. He looked Jameson in the eye, then he turned and walked away, angry and confused. He heard Jameson's laughter as he retreated. He turned and shook his fist at him. Jameson smirked at him.

His former page appeared at the edge of the crowd, waving to him. She ran up to Morrow with a ready smile.

"Don't worry. We've already got a campaign started to reelect you." Ja'wauna Davis grinned her characteristic bright grin, full of hope and a can-do attitude.

She'd grown up in the hood and knew what adversity could do to people's spirits. She'd vowed to get out, and she did by attending college and by getting a degree in law so that she could fight for what she felt was right. She had encouraged Morrow to stand firm with Representative John Lewis in the battle for voting rights. He admired John Lewis more than anyone in Congress for his love of peace and for his nonviolent protests in the deep South. That he had his skull cracked open during a protest endeared him even more to Morrow. Ja'wauna simply adored Lewis; he was an icon. She loved the former senator Walter Morrow too for his staunch support of West Virginia's split from the Confederate state of Virginia. She knew some of Morrow's ancestors had shed Union blood to free her ancestors. She also knew that, although he was humble, he would stand strong for human rights, especially for civil rights. That Mrs. Morrow was an attorney who defended those whom she felt hadn't gotten a fair shake, and whose grandmother was Black, also endeared the Morrows to Ja'wauna.

Morrow appreciated Ja'wauna's tenacity and quick wit.

"You're the one who should run for office. I'm too old to start over in six years, but you'll be just the right age. Come to my house, and we'll talk about it. I'll back you 100 percent."

Ja'wauna and her friends frequented his home as a sanctuary that welcomed people of color. They often discussed civil rights issues into the wee hours of the morning. Morrow was no pushover.

"Okay, Senator. I sure appreciate the support. I'll do whatever I can for West Virginia and for America. You know that."

Dressed in a sharp Brooks Brothers suit, she looked every bit like an aspiring senator, but she knew the color of her skin would make it an uphill battle, the kind she'd fought all her life. Morrow beamed at her, brightening at the thought of getting a principled person elected.

Another figure at the edge of the crowd caught Jameson's eye, a beautiful stiletto-thin Black girl. Their eyes locked. Then she turned and spoke to a younger child. Jameson felt something stir in his groin.

Many of the voters had overestimated the power of Jameson's effusive charm, confidence, bright blue eyes, and ready smile. It disarmed those who would criticize his lack of experience. Former senator Walter Morrow was best known for his fastidious attention to every bill presented to the Senate, sympathizing with those he felt had been treated unfairly, especially working-class folk since he himself had come from a family and had worked in the shafts. He voted according to the dictates of his conscience. He also loved nature and worked hard to convince his colleagues to vote for clean mines that didn't pollute streams or the surrounding environment. He was working to advance carbon capture and the recycling of carbon dioxide into the atmosphere, the latest technology to help preserve the planet. His only flaw was that he had become so immersed in saving trees and streams that he had lost his seat to this much younger man who had a large reserve of big company owners in his pocket and who called the sitting senator's reputation into question for spending too much money on conservation rather than on pure profit. He also smeared him for having led a coal miner's strike many years ago, questioning his patriotism, which made the former senator's blood boil.

The older senator had been caught off guard, believing the people would appreciate his championing just causes; whereas, the glamour and high profile of the fresh-faced challenger flattered them as they themselves longed for a form of celebrity. They admired his ability to charm and thought perhaps he'd add prestige to their poverty-stricken state as being progress-oriented instead of as a coal miner's stronghold. Members of both political parties voted him in, holding their heads a bit higher as they felt more in sync with the America they saw on television every night.

The newly elected senator was not quite as he appeared, for though he had a buoyant demeanor and a ready handshake for the miners, he favored people who were born into a life of wealth and social privilege just as he had been. His parents owned some of the coal mines. His great-grandparents had owned slaves, something he knew but never spoke of unless he was at a secret Ku Klux Klan meeting. He judged people who were having a rough go of it to be of weak character. The hippie movement, in particular, annoyed him as he didn't like men with long hair; he thought they looked effeminate and weak. He found the women without makeup and with flowers in their hair unattractive and unlikely to make good, submissive wives. Confident women rather frightened him. He was glad that, with a slight recession in the late '70s, the hippie movement had flickered and was no longer considered to be a threat to the elite. He also resented the egalitarian ideals of the '60s. Morrow's choice of a Black page annoyed him, especially since he had carefully hidden his own ancestry.

Jameson looked at Morrow's rumpled suit and bad haircut. He withdrew his hand quickly, hoping he hadn't contracted the flu or worse. He wiped it on a handkerchief tucked into his Armani suit. It was his turn to speak at the podium in the Senate, so he turned and strode to the speaker's rostrum with a brilliant smile that bespoke confidence. Morrow stayed to hear him. So did Ja'wauna. She expected a brash, know-nothing, self-congratulatory speech. She'd overestimated Jameson.

After introducing himself in the ornate Senate chamber where the US Senate convened, Jameson looked out at the august body of mostly aging men with gray hair and stern looks wrought from fatigue, a tiredness that came from hashing out issues over and over while making little progress.

He cleared his throat, introduced himself as the newly elected senator from West Virginia, and started his speech about how he planned to improve the welfare of the state, especially of its banking sector. His throat got a bit dry, so he took a sip of water from a glass that a Senate page had set on the small table next to him. When he looked up, his eyes glanced over the Senate. He saw Morrow and Ja'wauna, who appeared to be laughing at him. Unnerved, he lost his place in the notes he was reading from. He blanched. Unable to think of anything to say without his notes, he was lost. With a giggle, he started to sing "Mary Had a Little Lamb." The senators broke into peals of laughter, so he stopped, realizing that he had forgotten his speech and made a fool of himself. He gave Morrow a furious look and concluded quickly, saying something to the effect that he would make West Virginia the richest state in the Union. More laughter broke out. Jameson started to sweat, leaving the podium faster than he had approached it, determined to find Morrow and give him a piece of his mind; for he blamed him for his own faux pas. That was the nursery rhyme that the KKK sang to signal an attack.

He walked at a brisk pace to where he'd seen Morrow, but he couldn't find him. He didn't yet know where his own seat in the Senate was. Flummoxed, he turned to see the senators tittering with their heads together. Jameson couldn't stand humiliation, and he was thoroughly humiliated. Thoughts of revenge ran through his mind. He knew he had to do something significant and do it fast in order to impress the other senators. He would have to make sure his speech-writer came up with an outstanding speech for his next appearance in the Senate.

Morrow joined his plump, plainly dressed wife who had kinky blond hair held firmly in place by a lovely silver barrette with the American eagle on it and a determined look on her slightly pudgy face. She was waiting for him. She never went to beauty parlors or worried about her looks. She had gone to law school instead and fought for women's rights, civil rights, voters' rights; she loved the underdog. She knew how they suffered. Her grandmother had been Black, the child of a slave who had not had a kind master. Her husband loved her for her big heart and for her very warm feet during long winters when they cuddled under thick blankets. Ellie hugged him while Ja'wauna smiled. She helped them into their electric Tesla and waved goodbye. They drove home, dejected.

"I think this man is going to wreak havoc on our poor state. West Virginia has always stood for more than banking. We seceded from Virginia in 1861 because we thought slavery was inhuman. We may not be the richest state, but we have principles."

"There's a silver lining to every cloud," replied Ellie, who always tried to buoy her husband's spirits. "My next case deals with a woman who was wrongfully fired."

They drove on in silence, taking deep breaths to calm their spirits. She put her hand on his thigh to comfort him. They loved touching one another; simply being in her presence soothed his nerves. Morrow looked forward to taking a rest in the company of his family although he vowed to continue to work on behalf of workers' and voters' rights. They'd been hoodwinked one time too many. Jameson's election was the last straw. Morrow shifted into high gear as they entered the freeway and headed toward Mohegan, their small town in West Virginia. Ellie squeezed his thigh. He smiled.

Senator Jameson waited to speak with the other senators. He joked about his moment of levity during his speech as if it had been intentional. Those around him smiled and said that they had appreciated his jest—that it was a balm to their souls in these tension-filled times. He fell rapidly in step with the more conservative ones and soon found a committee he wanted to serve on called the Enhanced Living Standards Committee. This latter believed that the fewer children a family had, the more likely they were to remain out of the poverty bracket. The fact that many of the people from small families often became destitute and lonely later in life didn't concern them.

This committee's goal was to control population growth, especially among certain groups and races which they regarded as expendable, perhaps even dangerous. They thrived on paranoia.

Strictures against sterilization perplexed the young senator, and he was not alone. As he left the office one evening after he and the other members of the Committee for Enhanced Living Standards had delved into the subject of the world's burgeoning population, he quoted statistics that he knew by heart on how overpopulation contributed to impoverishment. The other members nodded their heads in agreement. The committee adjourned until the next week. Jameson pushed his well-padded chair away from the large oval mahogany table that had been taken from a tropical raintree forest.

As he descended the marble stairs from the Capitol, a shadowy figure approached him. He was one of the men who had listened to him in the meeting. He hadn't made much of an impression on Jameson because he wasn't wearing an expensive suit. It looked almost as bad as Morrow's.

"Hello, I'm Jack Smith of the Biological Warfare Laboratory in Fort Bener."

Senator Jameson turned and saw a man of slight build around forty with pale-gray eyes who proffered his hand. The senator shook it, looking down on the man because he was much taller than him.

"I heard you speak. You're working on the world's population explosion."

"You might put it that way," said Jameson.

The slight man stepped forward, trying to make himself taller by standing on his toes a bit, a habit he'd developed some years before. After all, shortness of stature was an undesirable trait.

"To speak frankly, we need your help in authorizing more funds for our scientific research that could help curtail this problem." He parted his lips to smile, but since he had a snaggletooth, he didn't show all his teeth. The result was a crooked smile.

Senator Jameson could tell from the man's bearing, by his manner of speech, and by his expensive cuff links that he was someone worth listening to after all. The cuff links outweighed his inexpensive suit in Jameson's estimation. The wind whipped through Jameson's blond locks.

"What kind of research?" Jameson's even teeth glistened in the waning rays of the sun as he smiled his bleach-enhanced, dazzling smile.

He also bleached his hair to look more Aryan. He considered his looks to be his biggest asset. They were.

"It has to do with population control and classified research," stated Smith.

His earnest, straightforward manner of speech and fashionable glasses gave him just the right combination of style and intelligence to appeal to the senator.

"As I'm sure you know, certain populations are not only undesirable but out of control."

He had already surmised that Jameson had a race-control mindset, or he wouldn't have shown such interest in a biowarfare lab. He knew the type.

At this moment, Morrow, who had lost the election but who still frequented Washington, D.C. appeared. He frowned at them and actually shook his finger at the scientist with such vigor that they both laughed at the older gentleman, who turned heel and walked away, muttering to himself.

Suddenly he turned around and walked up to Jameson, his face set with resolute determination. "You are a scurrilous cheat! You cheated at the polls, and you will cheat the hardworking citizens of West Virginia!"

Jameson's face contorted for just a moment. Then he gained control of his emotions and laughed at the older man.

"He's my former opponent." Senator Jameson laughed as he watched Morrow trudge away.

"Ah, yes, that's Mr. Morrow, a tedious workhorse. He's finished in Washington. At any rate, if you can convince the committee and Congress to vote sufficient funds for our research, I can guarantee you an effective way to control any population you like"—he chuck-led, his snaggletooth showing this time—"or dislike."

The two men exchanged grins. A kinship grew between them at that instant although Jameson noted that Smith's teeth would be a handicap if he were to speak to the committee.

"So be it," commented Senator Jameson. He nodded curtly to a female page who walked briskly by, noting her attractive figure. Then he smiled at the bespectacled man to whom he'd been talking. "I'll do my best."

Mr. Smith handed Jameson his card. "Jack Smith, Chief Executive of the Center for Biological Warfare" was inscribed on it. Jameson nodded in approval when he saw the importance of the man he'd been talking to. He hadn't wasted his time. They shook hands. Jameson smiled briefly and nodded. Then he turned abruptly and continued walking down Pennsylvania Avenue, a brisk wind keening his senses to the oncoming autumn.

He caught up with the curvy young page who'd walked past him.

"Good evening," he said, touching her arm.

She turned and said, "Good evening, Senator."

"Would you like to stop at the Plow and Angel for a quick update on the Beltway political gossip?"

His blue eyes sparkled, excited by her lovely perfectly oval-shaped face, the kind he preferred, not to mention her agreeable hourglass figure.

"Not tonight. I've got work waiting for me at home," she said.

"Perhaps another time," he murmured, doffing his hat in a show of respect. He liked to be thought of as a gentleman.

She smiled slowly. "Yes, I do enjoy talking politics," she said as she turned and walked quickly away.

Mr. Morrow watched from a discreet distance, frowning and swearing under his breath. "Cheating the good people," he murmured.

Jameson looked back at him briefly. "He'll regret that insult," he muttered. "No one calls Senator Jameson a cheat and gets away with it."

Thoughts of revenge coursed through his mind as his blood pressure rose. But he had bigger fish to fry, namely the funds to develop deadly bacteria which were resistant to antibiotics for those whose immune systems were compromised either by poverty or by age. He considered poor people and people of color to be inferior, and poor whites were beneath his contempt. As for the elderly, they were expendable.

When Senator Jameson proposed that the funds be made available for the Center of Biological Warfare to develop an antibiotic-resistant vaccine as a means of protecting the country from its most egregious enemies, his ideas were met with dissenting views. Only a few senators nodded their approval. Nonetheless, several million dollars were approved for the project. Senator Jameson's presentation to the committee the next day went smoothly despite his unsubtle manner, paving the way for the development of a biological agent to eliminate enemies.

By 1998, the scientists at the biowarfare laboratories had developed an antibiotic-resistant microbe/virus known as GIA. Mr. Smith communicated this discovery to Senator Jameson, already somewhat thickened at the waistline from being wined and dined on the Beltway for the past few months.

"We need a human test population," he said.

Jameson gave him a penetrating look and mentioned Haiti, which had such poverty and political corruption that Haitians were seeking asylum in the United States.

"We wreaked havoc on the gay populations in New York, San Francisco, and Los Angeles in the late '70s by injecting them with HIV. We told them it was a hep C vaccine. Almost all of them died. Some doctors got suspicious and tried to expose us but we got away with it. We could experiment on the immigrant Haitian population." Smith's wan face contorted in a contemptuous sneer. Then he laughed. "Just leave it to me," he said with a hint of a smile.

His cell phone beeped; he took the call, walking away from Jameson so he couldn't overhear anything. Putain was on the line. Jameson nodded, and they parted ways.

As he walked down the steps to the Capitol building, he saw the elderly Mr. Morrow. He knew that he had labored assiduously on human rights bills, especially workers' rights. Ja'wauna made sure he strengthened voters' rights. Jameson planned to pay lip service to such bills, which usually died in committees that had other priorities. A look of disdain came into Jameson's eyes when the former senator looked at him. Morrow's disheveled suit and white hair disgusted the senator. He considered him a sorry excuse for a human being. A look of furor came into the old man's eyes as Jameson turned and walked quickly away from him without acknowledging his presence. He got into his waiting limousine and told the driver to step on it. They sped away into the darkening evening, leaving Mr. Morrow on the stairs of the Congress building he'd once worked in.

Out of the shadows darted a heavyset woman with a determined look on her face.

"I've got some evidence," she said.

Her wavy dark hair blew across her face as a stiff breeze picked up. She brushed it away, straightening the skirt of her businesslike suit.

"Fort Bener has developed a virus that weakens human resistance to antibiotics." She halted, staring away. "They're talking about a new disease."

Morrow's jaw dropped. This was more than he'd anticipated.

"Those with weakened immune systems, such as coal miners…
and the underclass that lives in poverty? Especially—"

"Yes, and others deemed socially unacceptable," she said. Her
chest heaved from the exertion of divulging information that could
put her in danger.

They exchanged nods.

"I'll speak to the other senator from West Virginia about this."

The heavyset woman turned and walked briskly away. Morrow
watched her go with a look of concern on his wizened face. Then
he turned around and walked slowly down the steps of the Capitol
Building.

Senator Jameson had a meeting scheduled with Jack Smith the
next day. He drank his coffee that morning while going over a briefing.

"Anything of note?" asked his Russian-born wife, still girlish
and trim, but no longer in her twenties, as she placed a plateful of
scrambled eggs in front of him.

He gave her an impatient look, annoyed that she'd interrupted
his reading. He'd married her for her beauty, not her brains.

"Just a brief. Have to meet with someone from the Biological
Warfare Department today."

Svetlana narrowed her brown eyes. "Sounds contagious." She
tried to laugh but couldn't as the thought of the Biological Warfare
Department infuriated her.

"You know better than to make one of your wisecracks while
I'm thinking!"

She turned her head, blond hair coiffed in a neat bun, and
coughed. "Well, after all, a wife has the right to get a word in edge-
wise from time to time."

"Stop drinking that feminist Kool-Aid. Just because you're a
doctor—"

"Precisely, because I deal with bacteria on a daily basis. The very
idea of experimenting with germs that should be extinct—"

Jameson stood up abruptly, spilling his coffee. "It's top secret.
I never should have told you. I'm already under a cloud of suspicion
because I married a Russian."

Svetlana stood up from the breakfast table, put her dishes in the sink for the maid, and put on a figure-hugging coat.

"Would you like a divorce?" she said as if she'd asked him to pass the eggs.

She allowed her Russian accent to get thicker.

Jameson smiled at her. She always looked distinguished in that coat.

"Oh, Svetlana! Let's not argue. No, I don't want a divorce!" He paused, upset that she'd mention a divorce. "Sveta, you know I love you." He tried to smile.

"I don't want you to get into trouble...or to catch a disease! I have a patient at nine. I'll see you at dinner."

She leaned over. He smiled up at her lovely face. Then he kissed her hard on the lips. She pulled away, annoyed by the brusqueness of the kiss. She had a bruise on her thigh from where he'd kneed her when she refused to accommodate his ever-increasing sexual demands last night.

"Dinner at eight. I may bring someone from Fort Bener with me."

Svetlana rolled her eyes. "I can hardly wait."

She walked out the front door at a brisk pace, wondering why she'd married such a status-hungry beast. She had begun to detest him the moment he had belittled her for being a doctor instead of a dutiful wife. The two were not mutually exclusive. She wondered why he was so interested in bacteriological warfare. As a doctor, she hated the very thought. Her thoughts went to her fifteen-year-old daughter in Russia.

Svetlana grimaced. *How am I going to get Bill to allow me to bring her here? Even adopt her?*

She shut off her thoughts as much as she could because, if she started grieving over her first husband, she'd end up crying and getting nothing at all accomplished today. She buttoned her coat and left the house for the hospital.

*****

Jameson parked his late-model Mercedes in the Fort Bener parking lot. He checked his overcoat and jacket for lint, ran a comb through his already neatly coiffed hair, and got out of the car. He checked his watch and walked into the building in front of him at a brisk pace. He looked behind himself to make sure no one had seen him as he took the elevator to the fifth floor, where the bacteriological warfare meeting would take place.

Jack Smith waited for him, tapping his fingers on the long table with impatience. When Jameson walked in, he smiled with relief and nodded. Jameson nodded back and sat down next to him. Jameson amused him with his intense interest in biological warfare.

"Are you ready?" asked Jack.

"I'm always ready," said Jameson with an insouciant look that he felt would intimidate Smith.

Jack Smith laughed too loud, attracting some attention from the other biologists already sitting at the table.

"This is Senator Bill Jameson," said Jack.

The biologists nodded at him. Some felt nervous because senators rarely took an interest in biology.

"He's interested in our work for the good of the country," said Jack.

The others mumbled something to the effect that it was an honor to have a senator come to Fort Bener, but many felt something was amiss although they said nothing.

Jameson smiled as the presenter walked into the room. He took notes during the bacteriological warfare meeting. When it was over, he walked over to Jack Smith.

"Would you like to have a drink?"

Jack smiled at the handsome senator; he surmised that he wanted some extracurricular action. He liked women and booze too, so he smiled a broad snaggletoothed grin.

"We can go to the Gridiron Club. It's very elegant...and quite private there."

Jameson smiled his approval. They chatted about a new nerve drug as well as the antibiotic-resistant bacteria that were being developed at Fort Bener as they walked briskly to the Gridiron Club, noted for being a male bastion. Women had gotten the right to join a few years ago but rarely used the privilege, preferring staying in their offices to work. Out of the corner of his eye, Jameson saw Morrow shaking his fist at him. He was with a Black congresswoman. At least he thought it was Morrow. He shook his head, trying to clear his mind. He ignored them to focus on the man from Fort Bener, Jack Smith.

Comfortably seated in plush leather armchairs, he and Jack Smith leaned forward over their scotch and sodas.

"What of this nerve agent you mentioned?"

Jack looked surprised. "What of it? Nerve agents are nothing new."

He frowned at Jameson because he wasn't supposed to divulge information about what the scientists at Fort Bener were working on, but Jameson's august good looks and the scotch and soda had taken effect. He began to talk in earnest.

"We've developed a nerve suppressant that works so fast and is so deadly that it can kill in an instant and without a trace." Somewhat shocked at what he'd said, he took a swig of his scotch, which relaxed him. "The Russians have something similar."

Jameson leaned even closer to Jack Smith such that Mr. Smith felt a frisson of intimacy. An almost sexual excitement came over him. He enjoyed the company of attractive people.

"Could you obtain a sample for the committee? Or for me? This sounds very effective."

Jack Smith inhaled deeply, wondering how he could do this. Perhaps he could give him something fairly benign but poisonous. He wanted to cultivate his friendship; a senator could help him attain his superior's ultimate goal. Smitten by the august power of such a fine-looking senator, he nodded his head, unworried of the consequences of releasing a lethal drug.

Jameson grinned at him and nodded his head. "I can't thank you enough. This will help the committee more than you can imagine. I'd prefer something on the order of AIDS, only faster acting." He snapped his fingers in the air. "Waiter, another scotch and soda, on the double!"

The Black waiter looked at him with slight consternation. He hated men who ordered him around as if he were a robot. He couldn't stand these tony types, their sense of entitlement, and bad manners, but he had to make compromises to keep his job. He got the drinks.

He put them in front of the two men who were, by now, huddled together like Siamese twins. Jameson had even put his arm around Jack Smith's shoulders. He took the drink, ignoring the waiter. He and Smith continued to drink, talking and laughing all the while. The waiter muttered something inaudible under his breath.

*****

At Columbus Hospital, Dr. Jameson watched a young male patient's cardiac monitor flatline. She took his pulse and shook her head.

"No determinable cause of death," she said to the nurse.

He wrote her words onto the patient's chart. "What the?" he mumbled.

"I'd like to have an autopsy to determine the cause of death," she said, taking off her white laboratory coat.

"Yes, Dr. Jameson. I'll have it done right away."

"As soon as possible," she said, picking up her navy-blue woolen coat and buttoning it. She smiled and turned a spiky stiletto heel. "Thank you."

As Svetlana filed out of the crowded restaurant as fast as her ultra-high stilettos would allow, she saw a face from the past and began to run, tripping over a waiter's foot. She fell onto the carpeted floor with a loud ouch. The waiter helped her to her feet. She flashed a furtive look at the face that had shot panic into the core of her being. He stood and walked in her direction. Panic hurled her out the door to the street.

She jammed her car ticket into the valet's hand, looking nervously around for the face that had terrified her. The valet brought her Mercedes-Benz in front of the awning that led to the elegant restaurant. She pushed a couple of dollars into his hand and slid into the driver's seat. She spun the wheel around and pointed the car into the busy street, almost hitting another car, which slammed on its brakes to avoid hitting her.

"Calm, calm, calm," she chanted to herself in Russian, trying to regain her composure.

It was no use. There was someone in the back seat with a gun pointed at her.

"What do you want?" she said in Russian.

"You know what we want, Svetlana Sergeievna. Loyalty, obedience, and a good, trustworthy comrade. We gave you everything, and you defected."

"I had no choice."

"*Nyet.* You always had a choice. You defected from the Soviet Union. Now you pay the price."

Svetlana could see the man's pale face in her rearview mirror. She recognized him from when she'd worked for the KGB as a double agent. His eyes had pouches under them. His face was lined, but it was Boris.

She counted to ten and crashed the car into a telephone pole. The gun misfired, leaving bullet holes in the dashboard. The steering wheel had her pinned to her seat, but she twisted to try to grab hold of the gun. She saw Boris tossed halfway out of the window; he hadn't been wearing a seat belt. She breathed deeply, trying to calm herself, knowing the police would arrive within minutes. Boris groaned. He had a head wound and some gashes from the glass where he'd hit the car window.

The police and paramedics arrived and took charge. What she didn't realize was that she'd hit a pedestrian when she turned the wheel to ram the telephone pole. She recognized him as a familiar face, a friend of someone who had introduced her to her husband, had helped her become a citizen of the United States, and had expected favors in return. He wanted her to find ordinary Russians in the United States who were not really ordinary, who were tracking down spies who might also want to defect. Those spies would regret giving any secrets to the CIA. She knew this, yet she felt obligated to the man who'd helped her. He was a friend of the man who'd just been ejected halfway out of her car and was groaning. Beads of sweat formed on her forehead. She heard a siren and breathed a bit more easily.

The police jumped out of their patrol car and charged to the scene of the accident.

"Could I see your driver's license?" The burly Black policeman shifted his weight with his hand clenched, ready to go for his gun if necessary.

She looked up at him in the midst of the chaos of more police arriving, paramedics placing her injured passenger onto a gurney, and a crowd of people gawking at them. They helped the pedestrian to his feet. He was shaky but managed to walk. She felt paralyzed with fear, looked for her purse, and saw it wedged between the emergency brake and the cradle for the emergency brake. Eyes wide with fear, she jerked at her pocketbook with no success. She looked up at the officer, who shifted his weight and asked her to show her driver's license again.

Svetlana tore open her purse, ruining the expensive leather, and spotted her wallet, which she grabbed like a life raft. She tugged the license out of her wallet and gave it to the officer, who examined it.

"You're a doctor?" he asked.

"Yes, a specialist," she said.

"Why didn't you help your passenger?"

The policeman peered into her face. He wondered if she'd shown him a fake driver's license or, worse, a stolen one, stolen from a doctor. He frowned at her.

Svetlana opened her eyes wide. "I...I don't know. I think I'm in shock. I was pinned in by the steering wheel." She ran her hands through her hair and teared up a bit.

"Okay. You had a nasty accident." He looked over at the paramedics who were administering first aid to the bleeding passenger. "Could you take her to the ER too? She's in shock."

He got her out of her car and helped her into the paramedic vehicle. She sat next to the driver while they gave first aid to the man who had accosted her. She turned and peered into his unconscious face. She shivered.

"I'm going to call my husband," she said, taking her cell phone out of the pocket of her suede jacket. Then she remembered the autopsy. "I also need to obtain some autopsy results of one of my patients."

Her husband's sudden interest in bacteria to control certain populations made her blood run cold. She wondered if he had anything to do with the assault tonight. As a former spy, she suspected everyone and had learned that one's closest friends and relatives could turn into murderers.

She dialed Jameson's number, but he didn't pick up. All she could do was leave a message telling him to call her at the ER of Columbus Hospital in Washington, D.C.

Chapter 2

Walter Morrow turned his car into his driveway and got out to open his garage door. He furrowed his brow and groaned; his back hurt when he opened the garage door. He walked into his unpretentious two-story brick house and smelled beef stew.

"Ah, beef stew." He grinned at the thought of sitting down to dinner with his family.

His oldest daughter, Chrissy, appeared in the doorway of the living room. Spotting her father, she ran to him and kissed him on the cheek. She looked at her mother, who ran in from the yard when she saw her husband's car. Her frizzy blond hair blew in the brisk fall wind. Her lovely round face was lined with wrinkles from hard work, but she was still pretty. Time hadn't changed her natural beauty. Morrow attempted to pick her up, thought of his bad back, and kissed her on the forehead instead. His whirling days were over.

"I've got both of you at the same time! What a lucky man I am!" Morrow took Chrissy by the hand and said, "Let me look at you. It's been months since I last saw my angel, and you're prettier than ever!"

Chrissy's deep-brown eyes shone with pleasure. She loved her parents to the point of burning the candle at both ends to get good grades and to make them proud. She'd inherited kinky hair from her mom and her dad's down-to-earth good humor. She was proud of her inclusive family with its multiracial DNA.

"You've been working too hard again, haven't you?" she said with a colloquial accent common to the region of Appalachia they lived in. "Have you reinvented the wheel yet?"

They laughed. Morrow put his arms around her, and they hugged.

"You're the one burning the candle, what with your obsession about saving this darn ole planet!"

Chrissy looked her father in the eye. "We've got to plant more trees, forests and clean up the streams. And we've got to start using public transportation, quit using the fossil fuels like they were candy bars."

He smiled at her determination, nodding in agreement.

"Did you know that trucks use nine times as much energy to transport goods as trains?" She steeled herself for a rebuttal.

"Yes, sweetie. That was Ike's idea. He wanted to create more jobs for truckers. I know we could put them to work installing solar units, but right now, it's good to have a hot meal waiting for me," he said. Not wanting to leave Ellie out, he commented, "And a smart, beautiful wife like you, Ellie."

Ellie turned away, blushing and giggling. "Aw, Walter, you know I love Chrissy's cooking and her passion for saving the planet!"

Morrow looked for the evening paper, which was on his favorite easy chair, old and worn but as comfortable as they come. The matching sofa sagged a bit, but they never thought about buying a new one. They loved their home and everything they'd worked hard to furnish it with. All that mattered to them was that it was theirs. Morrow smiled as he plopped into the easy chair and opened the paper.

"Those darned old corporations passed another law against labor unions. We need laws that help workers and the planet. I worked hard for that while I was a senator."

Chrissy nodded her head. "And this new guy doesn't give a hoot."

"Don't worry about nothin', Daddy. I've fixed the best beef stew you've ever tasted," yelled his other daughter, Sojourner, from the kitchen.

"Is that you, Soj?" Morrow got out of his easy chair. "Been hiding from me like when you were little?" He chuckled, his deep baritone voice making a pleasant booming sound.

"Yes, it's me, Daddy! I'm home on a break from that fancy Ivy League college ya got me goin' to. I like it there though even though most of the kids aren't from coal-mining families."

Their youngest daughter, who had come home for a visit from her studies in geology at Vassar, joined them. She had a lovely oval face lit up by a radiant smile. Her hair was thick and black, worn long and straight. Her skin was perfection incarnate, clearer than her older sister's with freckles she loved.

"Daddy!" She ran to his open arms and hugged him. She knew she had the world's best dad.

"Are you still working on your climate change thesis?" He grinned a grizzled, warmhearted grin.

"Would I ever stop? I've been studying the latest methods to develop clean energy from driving electric cars like Mom's to riding electric bicycles. We've got to stop warming the planet. Pretty soon, Mother Nature will react. Pollution and leaded water don't make for smart, healthy kids. Viruses thrive in heat. The glaciers are melting, and the seas are rising. We could have a pandemic—" She gasped for air, winded by her outburst. Her normally smooth brow was furrowed. Her hands were on her hips.

Morrow knew how passionate his daughters were about turning global warming around and helping every creature that ever crawled the earth.

He stood up and tried to whirl her around for fun. "Ouch! Darned old back just went out!" He put his hand on his lower back and limped a bit to make light of his bad back.

Morrow pulled out a chair for Ellie and motioned for his daughter to take a seat at the dinner table as well.

"That sounds promising. I want to hear every bitty detail!"

Ellie brought a steaming bowl of stew from the kitchen, grinning as if it were from the *Cordon Bleu*.

"My girls sure can cook!" She looked at them with pride.

"Let me help you," said Chrissy, standing up to lift it out of her mother's hands. She placed it on their sturdy, wooden dining room table that sat six. "After all, you were at the women's rights meeting most of the day."

Morrow looked up and smiled. "Soj is following in her mom's footsteps and doing her bit to advance women's rights in West Virginia."

Soj made a little bow with a sweet smile on her face.

"She thinks climate change is going to do us in," said Chrissy, frowning.

Ellie and Walter Morrow exchanged quick looks. They didn't want their daughters to argue over anything this evening.

"Pshaw," said Ellie with an embarrassed grin. "Wally, you know darned well you had a lot to do with helping us get those women elected to the state Senate."

"Didn't do a thing other'n vote for 'em. You always say that." Morrow lifted his head a bit higher, proud of his activist wife.

Ellie had studied law with a scholarship to cover the tuition fee. She decided to join progressive groups and work for miners' and everyone's rights. She knew everyone should get a fair shake despite what those who coveted power instead of the common people's well-being kept preaching. Child trafficking worried her night and day, but she knew better than to ruin a good dinner with talk about abused children. She also knew everyone agreed with her.

They sat down, said a hasty grace, and passed the stew.

As they passed the beef stew around, Chrissy said, "Daddy, they're turning old coal mines into solar energy plants in Germany. It doesn't take a lot of money, just know-how. We can do it here! We can train the miners to become technicians."

Morrow smiled at her fondly. "If only we could get the coal companies' CEOs to agree."

She stood up to ladle more stew into his bowl just to show that she loved him. "I've met one of them at the university. Perhaps you could talk to him."

Morrow looked down at his food. "I'm no longer a senator, sweet pea. But I'd be willing to talk to anyone."

"I mean to cool him down. Mom already gave him a piece of her poker-hot mind."

Everyone laughed, knowing full well how angry Ellie could get when it came to politics.

Still laughing, Morrow eyed a juicy piece of beef and ate it with appreciation. "You gals make the best beef stew in town!" He grinned at his wife across the table.

"That CEO can stew in it!" said Ellie.

Her daughters giggled.

"Give him my regards next time," said Morrow with a quick wink.

There was a knock at the door. Morrow pushed his chair back from the table, got up, and walked over to the door to open it. A worried Black woman in her late twenties with two small children looked up at him.

"Sorry for the intrusion, sir, but my husband was hurt right bad in a mining shaft accident, and…"

Her little girls stepped in front of her mother and said, "We've heard you're so very kind, and we're so very hungry."

Their sweet young faces tugged at the heartstrings of both Walter and his wife.

Ellie stood up and walked over to them. "My girls just made a nice big stew. I think there's enough for everyone."

Tears welled up in her eyes as she knew the suffering the under-paid miners and their families had to endure. The little girls had already won her heart.

"Yes, there's plenty for everyone! We'd be honored to have you at our table," rejoined her husband.

Chrissy beamed at them from the table although she knew it meant that her discussion with her father about clean coal would be set aside.

"How bad off is your husband?" asked Ellie.

"Things have changed now that that city slicker new senator is in charge," said the woman. "The company union hasn't got enough money set aside for hurt miners, and Charley's leg is hurt pretty bad."

"We're going to fight those changes. Don't you worry, my dear," said Morrow, taking the hand of the younger child, a five-year-old, in his and leading her and her mother to the table.

The eight-year-old sister clung to her mother's skirt and followed.

"But we've such a nerve intrudin' on you like this," stammered the mother, embarrassed.

"No needs be! I want to hear about the conditions in the mines and all these changes," said Morrow as he got an extra chair for her to sit on.

Ellie went into the kitchen and brought out extra plates for them.

"Tell me about how conditions have changed," he asked the visitor as he filled her plate with stew.

"We can't see the doctors when our kids are sick anymore... and my husband's been out on the street begging since he had his accident down in the shafts."

Morrow's face reddened. "Out in the streets? Begging? He should be compensated for his injury and treated by the doctors!"

"That's what we think, but all of a sudden, they won't do any- thing for us anymore. It changed overnight with the election. My family took us in, but Charley still tries to pay his way, even if it is by beggin'." She put her head down, ashamed of what she had just said.

Ellie looked at her in distress. "I'm going to do something about this! Could I see your husband?"

The young mother began to cry, overwhelmed.

Ellie took her hand and rubbed it. "Don't worry. We love to help miners. Wally used to be one himself. We won't let you be mis- treated! Now where is your husband?"

The woman blinked at Ellie. She'd heard about her selfless actions; she was known for them. Tears of gratitude began to flow down her cheeks.

"I'll take you to him after you eat."

Morrow smiled. "We're glad you came to us. You've suffered enough! I'm going to speak to my friends in Congress about this outrage. I know people who can help you, so they can't push you around."

"It's askin' too much, sir. I don't want to put you out of your way," she said with a trembling smile. "I know you folks busy pro- tecting people's rights and such."

Her five-year-old climbed into her arms; she resembled a *Madonna and Child*. Morrow noticed her almost celestial beauty; his heart went out to her.

"We want to help you!" His face clouded over, for this was news he dreaded, news of rich people profiting from the hard work of the miners and then not even taking care of them.

Ellie peered into her hardscrabble, world-weary face. She knew the hardships poor women endured, especially if they were people of color. "I consider it an honor to be able to help you, to drive you through this cold dark night to your home. I consider it something kin does for kin. My grandmother was Black."

The woman inhaled deeply. Tears formed in her eyes. "I know about your grandmammy, how she was a Black woman working for some recognition. Yes, we are kin. Won't you spend a minute once we get to my house? I got something I want to show you."

Ellie's heart accelerated. "I want to see everything you have to show me. I've been trying to get closer to my roots. I hope you can help me." She took a deep breath at the thought of a possible revelation.

The woman trembled. A person of Ellie's stature had never been in her home, a woman who had gone to college and was married to the former senator from West Virginia.

Morrow shoveled some stew into his mouth, tried to keep talking, and choked on a piece of meat. Distressed, he jumped up, gasping. Ellie ran to him and started pounding him on the back. She tried to administer the Heimlich maneuver, but it didn't work. Morrow couldn't breathe. He opened the door and ran out into the yard, gagging as he tried to spit out the meat. Ellie ran after him along with his daughters. They tried to turn him upside down on a swing set as he gasped for air. After a long choking session, he managed to spit out the meat that was strangling him. His face had turned bright red.

Chrissy dialed 911 for the paramedics. "Come quick. It's an emergency. My father's choking to death and turning bright red."

Morrow shook his head. He coughed hard. "No, no need. I'm all right. It's out now. I'm okay."

Chrissy stared at him. "Daddy, you're bright red. Let me take your pulse." She grabbed his hand and felt his pulse. "Daddy, I'm afraid you might be having a heart attack! Get some aspirin! If you chew it up, they say it will save your life!"

Ellie ran into the kitchen to look for the aspirin. She gave them to Walter; he chewed them up, making a face. Then she put her hands on his throat. He began to breathe regularly.

"Ellie, you've got the power to heal. I need to breathe. Let me walk around the yard."

Morrow's daughters grabbed him, holding him by his arms to make sure he didn't trip on anything. The woman and her two children came out of the house. They stood by, not knowing what to do.

A loud siren announced the paramedics' arrival. They jumped out of their vehicle and charged toward Morrow. One of them looked down his throat with a flashlight.

"It seems to be clear."

"I'm okay now. I spit it out."

The paramedics looked at him, trying to figure out what to do. "Please roll up your shirt sleeve. We need to take your blood pressure."

A paramedic helped Morrow roll up his shirt sleeve so that he could apply the blood-pressure cuff. "Don't talk. Just try to breathe normally."

He watched the blood pressure valve. It was sky high.

"Your blood pressure is 185/95. Are you sure you don't want to go to the hospital?"

Morrow took a deep breath and forced himself to breathe slowly. "It's nothing. It will pass. Just a piece of meat that went down the wrong way."

"Whatever you say, Senator Morrow, but it would be wise to spend a night under observation."

Morrow took several deep breaths, considering his options. He was no longer young, and that was a very high blood pressure. Perhaps they were right.

Ellie pressed his hand in hers. "I think you should go, Wally. Just to be on the safe side, ya know? I'd feel much better if you did."

Morrow bowed his gray head and nodded. "I guess you're right, honey. I'll do it to calm your fears. It won't hurt to spend a night under a good doctor's care." He stood up and nodded at the waiting paramedics. "Okay, boys. You know more about medicine than I do. I'm your pigeon."

They laughed, and he lay down on the gurney that they had already brought from the paramedic van. Ellie, Chrissy, and Sojourner kissed him goodbye on his cheeks. They were shaken.

"We'll come to get you in the morning," whispered Ellie with a tear trickling down her cheek. She couldn't bear the thought of losing him even though he wasn't in any apparent danger.

The paramedics reassured her that he was in the best of hands and started to whisk him away.

"He's still our senator, and we don't want anything to happen to him. He has to win the next election!"

Morrow coughed hard, and they laughed as they wheeled him into the paramedic van on the gurney.

Ellie and his daughters waved goodbye as the impoverished coal miner's family looked on, aghast.

Then Ellie grabbed the injured miner's wife by the hand and piloted her toward her Tesla. "Hurry. Maybe I'll be in time."

Soj and Chrissy jumped in their car.

"I don't know how to thank you, ma'am."

"Pshaw. I'm just trying to help a poor soul."

She started driving like a woman possessed to where the miner sat on an old wooden bench downtown. Ellie jumped out of the car and felt his leg. He looked surprised until he recognized her by her frizzy blond hair. Ellie was well-known among the miners.

"It's my knee. I can't walk on it." He stared at her and perceived a glow around her face. "You're an angel," he said as she pressed his knee, manipulating it with expertise.

Ellie knew the bones and sinews of the body from countless broken bodies she'd tried to fix. Most had to be taken to a hospital for treatment that their insurance didn't always cover.

"How do ya feel?"

He touched his knee, bent it, and stood up. "My Lord in heaven, I can stand!" He took a few steps forward with Ellie on one side and his wife on the other. "I can walk!"

"No, just a chiropractic manipulation I learned a long time ago when other miners were hurt. I think you'll be all right. Do you want to go home?"

His wife hugged Ellie close. Then she kissed her husband. "We've been staying with my family until he can work again."

Ellie walked back to her car and opened the door for the still-limping man.

"Thank you, ma'am. Thank you kindly! How can I ever repay you?"

Ellie laughed. "No need. Your recovery is payment enough. Now where's your house? My grandparents had troubles like yours."

The grateful mother smiled at Ellie. Your grandmammy was Black. You must know what we go through."

"She sure was, and a great woman who fought for miners' and Black people's, all people's, rights. Her mother was a Black suffragette, Black women just as powerful as white ones, and I'm a bit of both!" Ellie hugged her. "If ya need help, always call on us. Now where's your house? And what's your name?"

"It's Adelaide." She grinned at Ellie. "Our house, my parents' house, isn't far from the mines," she said, smiling so hard her gums showed. She was overcome with joy.

Ellie smiled back at her and gestured for everyone to get in her car. It was a squeeze, but they got in and put on their seat belts, laughing and happy with relief. Ellie gunned the engine and drove toward their house.

After driving along a dark, windy road, Adelaide exclaimed, "There it is! That's our house."

The house was dilapidated, hardly more than a shelter from the elements, but there were well-tended rose bushes along the stone path to the timeworn front door.

Adelaide took the key to the front door out of a satchel, one she'd made herself. Once inside, she turned on a kerosene lamp, which cast an eerie light on the meager furniture. There was a sewing machine in the corner.

"I make clothes for myself and my family." She grinned for the first time, proud of her work.

The years of travail melted away. Her face was beautiful, almost angelic in the dim light.

"Won't you have a seat?" She motioned toward the timeworn sofa.

Ellie sat down with Adelaide next to her.

"You children go get ready for bed," she instructed.

They nodded but didn't budge. "We want to see... Show us the pictures!" They cuddled close to their mother, begging to stay.

"You got to promise to keep still and not interrupt me. I got things to say," said Adelaide.

The children giggled and nodded. Their father left the room to go to bed. His knee still hurt, and he had had his fill for the day.

Ellie and Adelaide smiled at the children's spirited reply. Then they peered at one another, searching for commonality. Adelaide recognized Ellie's kinky hair and full lips from a picture of one of her ancestors.

"What did you want to show me?"

Adelaide smiled. "Just a minute. I'll get it."

She got up and went into another room, emerging with her family scrapbook. She turned the weathered pages with reverence, showing Ellie pictures of babies and weddings, mostly black-and-white photos, going way back in time.

These were classic Black people's pictures, big smiles to mask the hardship that they endured. They were happy and ready to face whatever came their way.

Adelaide turned a page. A light-complected baby smiled out of its swaddling clothes. Her mother was light-complected too. Ellie peered at her, recognizing a resemblance between herself and the woman.

"Who was that?"

"That was my great-great-grandmammy from the Jameson plantation near Charlestown."

Ellie's eyes widened. "The Jameson plantation?"

"Yes'm. The Jameson family had a big tobacco plantation, lots of slaves. My great-great-grandmammy was one of 'em." Adelaide turned to Ellie, hoping for some trace of understanding.

Instead, Ellie grabbed the album out of her hands, turning page after page in a frenzy. "Do you think these people might be related to Bill Jameson, the man who beat my husband in the recent election?"

Her hands trembled as she held up a picture of a typical wealthy slave-owning family with two ebony-black slaves standing in attendance.

She looked up at Adelaide. "My grandmother told me we had darker relatives who were slaves on a plantation near Charlestown." She took a deep breath. "Maybe we are more kin than you thought."

Adelaide grinned a sly smile. "You've heard about how our blood got mixed, how the massa required more than just cotton pickin', plantation buildin', house cleanin'…"

Ellie nodded, urging her to continue. "My grandma was Black, but she wasn't ebony like a lot of Black folks." She stood up, ran her hands through her kinky blond hair as she paced around Adelaide's living room. "What do you make of this? Why was she lighter than other Black folks?"

Adelaide stood up, facing Ellie. "Far's we can tell, that light baby came from a slave…"

She turned and looked at her children, who were paying rapt attention. She took them by the hand, leading them out of the room.

"Now you get ready for bed. It's past your bedtime," she said.

"Aw, Ma, let us stay…"

"This isn't for children's ears. I'll tell you when you're older."

Adelaide turned, squared her shoulders, and walked back into the room with Ellie.

"That baby came from a forced union."

Ellie peered into her face. "Just what I suspected."

"They had house Blacks who sometimes had children with the massa, or the massa just took his pleasure. She started to tear up. "We don't really know since slaves weren't taught to read or write. We couldn't leave any written word behind, just stories passed on from one generation to the next, if we weren't sold to another master. The closest we can get to our ancestors is in the graveyard." She started to cry.

Ellie's face hardened. "Do you mean they had burial grounds for slaves?"

"We found one near the plantation." She sobbed. "Guess they buried their kin by the light of the moon and in danger of being whipped...or worse." She dried her eyes on the sleeve of her cotton dress. She took a deep breath. "But they left stones for markers. Sometimes they etched somethin' on a stone. We can't tell if it was a name because they couldn't write and didn't have much time before gettin' caught...but sometimes they left a tiny stone embedded in the marker, like amethyst or something of value...on the children's..." She started to cry in earnest.

"No dates."

"No, ma'am." Adelaide shook her head, tears streaming down her face. "My ancestors were buried like you'd bury a cat or a dog unless their kin managed to do it in a hidden spot in the dark of night."

Ellie put her arm around Adelaide's shoulder to comfort her. "Maybe we can at least honor them by making these burial grounds known."

Adelaide looked at her in disbelief. "Let them be! Otherwise, worse things could happen."

Ellie started to tear up. The two women sank down on the sofa. Ellie took the album and began to page through it in earnest. She was sure these were her Black grandmother's ancestors.

She stopped turning the pages and instead stared directly into Adelaide's eyes. "Promise me you'll take me to the slave burial place on the old plantation."

Adelaide took a deep breath. Her head shook a bit. She looked around her family home with all its poverty and resigned herself.

"I promise," she said.

"Tonight?"

She took a deep breath. "Aren't you tired?"

"I've got to see this burial ground. Some of my ancestors are buried there too. It won't take long, will it?" Ellie stared at the photo that resembled her.

Adelaide sighed. "I guess not too long."

Chrissy and Soj had been listening, wide-eyed.

"They're our ancestors too!" said Soj.

"We want to come with you," said Chrissy. "Please let us come with you." She gave her mother an imploring look.

Ellie took a deep breath, shifting her weight as she thought of all of them descending on the hidden burial grounds. She shook her head.

"Let us go first, sweetie," she said.

Ellie stood up, straightened her dress, and put her coat on. Adelaide stood up and walked toward the front door. Ellie smiled at her and followed. The girls ran to the door with them.

"Not this time," implored Ellie.

She hugged Soj and Chrissy to her bosom; she loved them so. They nodded their heads, dejected but respecting their mother's decision. They knew that going to hidden graveyards wasn't like going to a prom.

Adelaide got in Ellie's car. Ellie drove for a few miles to the outskirts of the old plantation.

When they came to a thicket of dense trees, Adelaide said, "It's in there. Not much to see."

"It's not what there is to see. It's…it's our ancestors and their untold stories."

Adelaide nodded her head as Ellie parked the car on the side of the narrow road, a road rarely traveled since they'd built the bigger highway nearby.

They got out of the car. Ellie took a flashlight from the glove compartment. A full moon lit their way, bright and beckoning. A tall grove of trees stood before them. Adelaide walked into it, and Ellie followed, shining the flashlight on the ground so they wouldn't trip.

After what seemed like about half an hour, they came to a clearing with different-sized stones in it. Most of them were small boulders, but some were smaller.

"This is it," said Adelaide.

She peered at the graveyard in reverence. Ellie peered at the rocks. She knew they must mark the gravesites. One, in particular, caught her attention because something glinted on it.

"Are these grave markers?" she asked.

"Yes'm," said Adelaide, already overcome with long-repressed emotions. "That one's my great-great-granddaddy's, maybe. We don't really know since they couldn't read or write, nothing except a few wavy lines inscribed on them."

"What about this one?" Ellie walked over to one with a smaller stone over it.

There was a fresh vase of flower next to it.

She gasped. "Someone's still tending this hidden graveyard!"

"Yes'm. It's sacred to us Black folk. Those are our ancestors who worked the tobacco fields and Lord only knows what else."

Ellie put her arm around her waist to comfort her. "What's that on this smaller stone? It's shiny."

"Sometimes they put a ruby or something precious on the children's graves." She started to cry. "Every now and again, people will put flowers or a precious jewel to honor them. But they don't know who's buried there."

Ellie shined her flashlight at the stone. "There's something etched onto this one."

"It's just chicken scratch. They never got taught how to read or write."

Ellie kneeled down and peered at it. "That's not chicken scratch! That's Arabic cursive! It says something!" She ran her fingers over it.

"Arabic?"

"Some of the slaves descended from slaves who knew how to read and write in Arabic, I'll betcha," said Ellie. "If they came from Nigeria or other Muslim countries, they knew how to read and write in their own language. Wally can help us find out!" She inhaled deeply. A tear trickled down her cheek. "They weren't illiterate at all. Some of them must've taught their children how to write Arabic."

"Maybe we can find out who's buried there." Adelaide inhaled deeply. "Oh, praise the Lord!"

Ellie bent over to touch the stone when they heard a noise coming through the thicket. It was the sheriff.

"What you ladies doing here in the middle of the night?" He couldn't believe his eyes.

"We're just...just having a look-see," quavered Adelaide.

"No harm in that," added Ellie.

She stuck out her hand, and he jumped back, drawing his gun.

"Put your hands in the air!"

"I just wanted to introduce myself," said Ellie.

The sound of heavy footsteps in the woods behind them echoed in their ears.

"What's that noise?" Adelaide put her hands over her head. "We didn't mean no harm," she said, her voice quavering in fear.

"There's nothing to be afraid of." Ellie raised her head with a resolute look in her eyes.

The sheriff guffawed. "Just some bears or critters..." He turned to see six hooded members of the Ku Klux Klan emerge from the other side of the graveyard.

Adelaide started to make a run for it. Ellie grabbed her.

"We'll stand our ground! Our dead and buried ancestors would have done the same!" She stepped forward, squaring her shoulders and narrowing her eyes. "What are these men doing here, Sheriff?"

The sheriff chortled and laughed out loud. "I might ask you the same thing."

Ellie stepped in front of Adelaide, standing between her and the sheriff. "It's your job to protect us, not to question us!" She put her hands on her hips. "Fine lot of nerve they have," she mumbled under her breath.

"What'd say?" asked the sheriff as the Klan members advanced toward them.

"These folks aren't exactly the Salvation Army," said Ellie in a louder than usual voice.

She was scared, but she didn't want to give them the satisfaction of knowing it.

The hooded Klansmen kept coming. One of them stumbled over a smaller gravesite marked by a stone with a shiny gem embedded in it, a child's grave.

"Ouch," issued from under his hooded presence.

The rock moved ever so slightly. Ellie felt faint. Her senses blurred as she thought she saw a form emerge from it, not human, but rather ghostlike.

The Klansmen screamed, "Watch out! It's one of them nigga babies coming back to get us!"

Everyone stood stock-still as the apparition wafted toward the Klansman.

"Your grandpappy took his pleasure with my mama and killed me when I tried to pull him off." The voice was eerie and otherworldly.

The Klansmen started to retreat.

"Now you gonna cut and run just like that massa did. But you can't hurt me now. And I got friends."

Ellie and Adelaide clutched each other in shock. The sheriff pointed his gun at the apparition and fired point-blank. Laughter emitted from its wavering form as it came closer to him.

"Bullets can't hurt me no more. Ain't nothing that can hurt me."

The sheriff dropped his gun and ran into the woods. Ellie picked it up. The Klansmen beat a hasty retreat toward the part of the woods they'd come from, but one of them stumbled over a bigger stone. It moved just like the child's headstone had. A larger ghostlike form emerged.

"You can't get away from your evildoing. We're coming after you. I was the one who tried to fight off the massa before he killed our child right before my eyes. You've got to mend your scurrilous ways. We want an apology. We want justice even if it is in the afterlife."

The Klansmen ran like the devil. The ghostlike figures followed them, wafting through the air, toward the plantation house, where their own graveyard lay behind a nearby church. They started screaming and begging for mercy, saying that they meant no harm. Some of them started to cry. The ghostlike forms moved faster until they reached the church graveyard. Adelaide and Ellie ran after them, hand in hand, unsure if they were imagining things or seeing ghosts from the afterlife.

The humble old Methodist church lay bathed in moonlight; its steeple pointed toward the heavens. It was a humble church built by slaves for their masters. After the Civil Rights Act passed and was signed into law, Black people joined them with fear and trepidation.

"That's where they used to pray," whispered Ellie as she staggered after Adelaide.

Adelaide nodded her head and laughed. "I wonder if they ever asked the Lord to forgive them for their trespasses, for their sins, because they sinned plenty."

She wiped her eyes with the edge of her shawl to dry a few tears that had trickled down her cheeks.

One of the tombstones started to rock back and forth. Adelaide and Ellie clutched each other, scared to death.

"Dear Lord!" gasped Adelaide.

A wraithlike ghostly form emerged from the tombstone with Jameson inscribed on it. This was a graveyard for white people.

"The Lord laid us to rest. Leave us in peace."

Ellie squealed in fright. Adelaide held her tight.

More wraithlike forms emerged from the other tombstones till about fifty of them faced the newcomers.

"You ain't got no business here," echoed from one of the wraithlike forms.

The forms from the hidden slave graveyard swooshed in front of it. "We got plenty of business here. We want justice even if it's been a long time coming."

The two groups faced each other, with Adelaide and Ellie in between quaking in fright, not knowing if they were hallucinating or imagining what they saw.

"You beat my great-great-grandmammy," ventured Adelaide. She turned and faced another wraithlike form. "Was you the one who lynched my great-great-grandpappy?" She let go of Ellie and shook her fist at it.

"They was our property. We had the right to do with them as we saw fit."

Adelaide lunged at the form. It retreated.

"Nobody is the property of another!"

The wraithlike form retreated a bit more, saying, "Slaves weren't human. They couldn't read nor write. We did as we pleased. You're lucky to be standing here today."

Ellie tried to restrain Adelaide as she ran toward the form.

"We gonna see the justice of the Lord God tonight!"

The other ghostlike forms advanced, chanting, "Go down, Moses. Go down, Moses…"

Adelaide sank to the ground and put her hands in front of her face. "Dear Lord, let there be justice for the sins committed against my people." She took deep breaths.

Ellie sank down next to her. "Yes, Lord, do unto them as you see fit."

The ghostlike forms sank to the ground in a form of reverent prayer.

A bright light illuminated the old church graveyard. The wraith-like ghosts shrank back.

"Don't hurt us!" they begged. "We meant no wrong. They's our slaves even in the afterlife."

The light grew brighter and brighter until Ellie and Adelaide had to cover their eyes. It was blinding.

The ground rumbled. A figure dressed in red with a pitchfork emerged as the land opened, revealing the pits of hellfire beneath.

The wraithlike forms huddled together, sinking to the ground.

"You've been rightfully accused and will pay the price, the after-life price."

It started to stab the wraithlike forms with its pitchfork and hurled them into the flaming pit. They screamed and begged for mercy. The ghostlike forms of the former slaves rose up in unison. One of them rose up and lay against a wooden cross that appeared.

"Forgive them," issued from its tortured mouth.

Everyone fell to their knees in prayer.

"Dear Lord Jesus, we most humbly beg thy forgiveness," said Ellie. "We sought justice for those so sorely mistreated."

She and Adelaide fell into a trance.

"Fear not, my child. Only the innocents are allowed to go to heaven and sit by the holy ones." It gestured toward the forms of the former slaves in their ghostlike forms. "These poor souls were buried in haste and fear. They deserved a proper burial and a eulogy. Now they shall have it."

"Hallelujah!" the ghostlike forms of the slaves shouted in unison and rose as in prayer.

An angel motioned for them to ascend. Slowly, surrounded by a white light, the forms ascended toward heaven. The other forms, the former massas and their relatives, vanished into their graves.

"And they shall remain in purgatory until they repent. But no man or woman is forced to remain in purgatory if they see the light."

Adelaide and Ellie clutched one another as they stared at the graves. "Praise be," they said, staring at the heavens.

The wraithlike forms receded, and all was silent and dark again.

Chapter 3

The starry night was crystal clear as the paramedics sped along the twisting, ill-repaired roads to the nearby hospital, only to be told that Morrow should be flown to a Washington, D.C. hospital that would be better equipped to give him a thorough workup.

"Don't go to so much trouble," Morrow protested.

But before he could blink an eye, he was in and out of a helicopter and lying comfortably on a hospital bed in Columbus Hospital.

A nurse entered the room and checked his blood pressure and pulse. "The doctor will see you in a few minutes. We're going to have to put another man in your room. I hope you don't mind." She looked at Morrow to see if he minded having another patient in the same room.

Morrow nodded his head and watched as two orderlies wheeled a heavyset man with platinum-blond hair in.

"This is Mr. Boris Bogomolov," said a nurse with tired eyes. "He's been in an accident."

"I'm sorry to hear that," said Morrow. "I hope his injuries aren't too serious."

The nurse said curtly, "The doctor will be in soon to talk to both of you." She had had to work a double shift and was exhausted.

"What kind of accident was it?" asked Morrow, concerned.

"He was ejected from a car. He wasn't wearing his seat belt." She shook her head as she took Boris's pulse.

"Such a pity. Everyone should buckle up," murmured Morrow, shaking his head in sympathy.

Boris opened his unbandaged eye and grunted. "I don't need any safety lectures right now."

Morrow smiled at him. "I didn't mean to offend you. I used to work on car safety bills when I was...when I was in the Senate."

Yelping in pain, which he'd been trying to conceal, Boris twisted his head to look at Morrow.

"Take it easy, my man. You've just been in an accident." Morrow coughed.

"You think I don't know that?" Boris stared at the older gentleman lying in the bed next to his.

"Well, yes," stammered Morrow, upset that he might have said the wrong thing to an injured man.

"Did you say you were in the Senate? Do you mean the United States Senate?"

Morrow nodded his head slowly. "I was until a younger man defeated me. I served my country for almost twenty-five years. I like to think I did a lot of good."

Boris appraised Morrow. "You don't look like a senator. Which state did you represent?"

Morrow looked at the injured man and decided he wasn't hurt too bad to tell him he didn't look like a senator. He felt miffed. Sadness crept into his heart like a dirge. Maybe that was why he'd lost. He didn't look the part. Beaten by a handsome younger man who cared nothing for the people of West Virginia. He cleared his throat with some difficulty.

"West Virginia, the proud state of the best coal mines in the country. We were getting them to produce clean coal, getting them up to environmental standards. I served for twenty-four years. I'm also proud to say we split from the state of Virginia in order to fight slavery."

Boris stared at this man. He'd never met a humble senator, much less one who had served so long yet looked like just about anybody. He had no stature, no gravitas. He reminded him of the old Communists he'd known in Russia. What's more, he talked about slavery as if the Civil War were a recent event.

"I'm sure you served your country well and fought for workers' rights. Coal mining is dangerous and dirty work. Do you know the man who took your place?"

"Not really. His name is Jameson. He doesn't seem to take the impoverished peoples' difficulties to heart, from what I can tell." Morrow cleared his throat again. "You have a bit of an accent. If you don't mind, may I ask what country you're from?"

"Russia." Boris smiled a crocodile smile when he heard him say Jameson's name. Here was a potential ally.

Morrow looked into his eyes with keen interest. He knew things had changed since Stalin and the eventual defeat of Marx-style Communism.

"I believe they take good care of their workers in Russia, if I'm not mistaken."

Although he didn't approve of most of the tenets of Communism, he admired the idea of the equality of the classes, the proletariat and such. He didn't approve of the violence advocated in Karl Marx's infamous treatise, *The Communist Manifesto*. He knew that, even though Russia wasn't really a Communist country anymore, they must nurture remnants of their former doctrines. Morrow nurtured his long-held belief that someone somewhere cared about the working class, about humanity.

"We do our best. It isn't a perfect system, but it works for us."

"Are there hungry people in the streets?"

Boris smiled a broad smile. Here was a man he could use. A bit of a patsy, but he had sympathy for the working class and seemed gullible. Thoughts whirled through his mind. He began to feel a bit dizzy. He closed his eyes. He wanted to avoid answering the homeless question.

Morrow sat up in his hospital bed, concerned.

"Are you all right? Doctor! We need a doctor!" shouted Morrow.

A few minutes later, a wizened old doctor walked into the room, his stethoscope at the ready.

"I'll be with you in a minute," he nodded to Morrow as he felt Boris's pulse.

Morrow held his breath for fear the man had died suddenly. He felt that he had talked too much and worsened his condition.

"I was talking to him when he suddenly closed his eyes, Doctor," said Morrow. "I hope I didn't do the wrong thing."

He smiled weakly at the doctor and cleared his throat, which still hurt from having had meat stuck in it.

The doctor smiled back at him. "Not to worry. It's best to let him rest for the time being. He's going to be all right. Now let me see your blood pressure results. I'm Dr. Mandel, by the way."

He stuck out his hand, and Morrow shook it.

"Yes, it shot way up tonight. That's why I'm here. I'm Walter Morrow. Nice to meet you."

The doctor nodded and looked at Morrow's chart. He furrowed his brow.

"Have you ever had chest pains or shortness of breath? Anything irregular other than getting a piece of meat stuck in your windpipe?"

"I don't think so, Doctor. I almost didn't come to the hospital, but my wife insisted. You know how wives worry." He chuckled.

Dr. Mandel nodded his head as he listened to Morrow's heartbeat through his stethoscope.

"Your blood pressure is high. I'm going to schedule some blood work and a treadmill stress test. If the results show you have high blood pressure, I'll prescribe a blood thinner." He smiled at the elderly man's kind face, which seemed to be listening to him intently. He patted his hand and said, "I think you're going to be fine. The phlebotomist will draw some blood. We'll let you know tomorrow, Mr. Morrow."

He couldn't resist making a silly jest, and Morrow laughed with him.

"People have fun with my name. I'm used to it."

"What about me?" growled Boris, coming back to life.

He turned his bandaged head toward them, trying to sit up.

"Your CT scan looks good. We're running more tests and will let you know as soon as we find out. You need to take it easy. Don't talk too much. Let your head wound heal. Try not to sit up. Just keep calm."

"We won't laugh at your name," Morrow said with a giggle.

He felt silly for some reason.

What's gotten into me? he wondered.

Boris frowned and then turned over in his bed, thinking that turning Morrow into an agent would be child's play. He'd get that bitch Svetlana yet.

Both men slept soundly and awoke early the next morning. Morrow was a bit confused at first, but then he remembered choking on the piece of meat. He wondered what the doctor would say about his blood test results, and he wondered about the man who shared his room.

Boris was a bit disoriented himself until Morrow gently reminded him he'd been in an accident.

"Oh, yes, that Jameson bitch," muttered Boris.

Morrow sat up in his bed and shook his finger at the bandaged head next to him.

"Don't ever say that! Women are our equals! In the case of my wife, our betters."

Boris sputtered and laughed. "She's a spy. Never trust a woman. She married that American rat as a cover."

"Spy? American rat? Jameson? Surely you're confused. Why, we have a senator named Jameson!"

Boris gave Morrow a dirty look from beneath his bandages. "That's the one."

Walter Morrow opened his eyes in shock. "Is Senator Jameson married to a…a woman who could be a spy? To tell you the truth, I'm not surprised. I don't trust him."

The hospital room suddenly seemed too small, too sterile. The white walls closed in on him. He wanted to go home.

Boris felt wide awake and smiled a toothy grin. "I couldn't agree with you more. She must be exposed."

A hefty nurse opened the door with a jaunty thrust and placed breakfast trays in front of them—orange juice, toast, and a poached egg. The coffee was black and hot.

"No cream for either of you due to your conditions," she said. Then she turned and walked out. She yelled, "Stay calm!" over her shoulder.

Morrow and Boris began to laugh.

"How's that for a warm bedside manner?" said Boris.

"A little humor never hurt," replied Morrow as he put some sugar in his coffee and took a sip. "The coffee's good."

"Delicious," chimed in Boris, determined to win Morrow over. "Would you like my egg? Can't stand eggs in the morning." He pushed his hospital tray toward Morrow with a big smile.

"Don't they eat eggs for breakfast in Russia?" asked Morrow, brimming with curiosity about the country of the czars, Marx and Engels.

He knew it had changed, but he wanted to know more. The idea of sharing a room with a Russian, from a former communist country, made his head spin. He'd met many important men, but they were all Americans. This man was different—very different, he'd soon find out.

"We just have toast and coffee."

"Don't your workers need hearty breakfasts?"

Boris grinned and tried to sit up. His head spun a bit, so he lay back down for a minute. He groaned and breathed deeply, turning toward Morrow again to try to cultivate his interest in Russia.

"We have many mines in Russia."

The image of President Putain speaking to miners in Siberia who'd written "Four months with no pay" on a roof to attract attention ran through his mind.

Bastards, he thought.

"What do your workers do? Oh, I'm making you talk too much! Please accept my apologies." Morrow realized Boris had a head injury, but he wanted to find out a few things from an actual Russian. "I'll let you have your breakfast in peace. Please tell me all about Russia when you feel up to it."

Boris grinned his crocodile grin at him. "Our workers are healthy and well paid. Russia reveres its workers. After all, we were once Communists and still hold Karl Marx in high esteem." He almost burst out laughing.

Morrow's eyes narrowed when he detected the smirk on Boris's face. For the first time in his life, he felt suspicion run through his mind.

"Our miners suffer from long hours in the dangerous shafts, and when there is a cave-in and they're injured...or killed...there is often no compensation." Morrow's wizened face contorted as he thought of the cave-in that had killed his father many years ago.

"I would like to know more after my head heals." Boris smiled. He smacked his lips together and grinned, thinking he'd struck a rich mother lode of information in this idealistic former senator. "Perhaps I can help."

"Thank you. I appreciate your concern," said Morrow, wondering how this man had gotten his head wound.

A former American senator who cares for others? Thoughts of cupidity ran through Boris's mind. He made a mental list of how he might use this man to Russia's advantage.

They heard the door open and looked up to see an elegant woman dressed in the latest Prada pantsuit and elegant heels under her white doctor's coat. It was Svetlana, her composure restored after a good night's sleep.

Boris stiffened. Morrow looked confused.

What is Senator Jameson's wife doing here? he wondered.

No one had told him she was a doctor.

Svetlana noted the elderly man in the hospital bed next to Boris, closed the door, and pulled up a chair to speak to Boris.

"Excuse me while I speak to this gentleman," she said, nodding her head at Morrow.

"Yes, of course. Don't let me get in the way."

Svetlana pulled the blue curtain that separated the two beds so that Morrow couldn't see her.

She lowered her voice and spoke in Russian, "How are you, dear Boris?" She smiled at him.

He was astonished. He'd just tried to kill her. What was she trying to do?

"What a shame I ran into that tree."

"I'm sure the tree agrees." Boris smiled, thinking she intended to silence him or pull some devious trick.

She looked over her shoulder to see if Morrow was listening to them. All was quiet, so she continued speaking in a barely audible voice.

"You should have fastened your seat belt, silly boy! It's the law here. And playing with that silly gun! What got into you? When it went off, it startled me. That's why I lost control of the car and ran into a tree. I'm sorry you were injured." She reached out to touch his bandage.

Boris grabbed her hand. "Did you report it to the police, my dear fellow Russian?"

"I had no choice, but they understood that your gun misfired. and it was all a nasty accident. This never would have happened in Russia," she hissed, releasing her hand from his grip. "You're going to be all right, of course!"

"Naturally, my dear Sveta. We Russians are tough. We survived Stalin, didn't we?"

"Yes." She feigned laughter. "Most of us...and who is the gentleman in the adjoining bed?" She motioned toward Morrow's bed.

"Open the curtain, and it will be my great pleasure to introduce you." Boris sneered at her.

Svetlana stood up and slid the curtain back. A flicker of recognition came over her face.

"Oh, Walter Morrow! How did you end up here?"

An almost electric shock ran down her spine. What could her husband's former opponent be doing in a bed next to a Russian spy? She shivered.

Morrow smiled at her. "I've been learning how well you treat your workers in Russia. Boris has been educating me." He nodded toward Boris and grinned with a glint of mischief in his eyes.

Svetlana gritted her teeth and tried to think of something to say. "Oh, how good of him. I think you know I'm a doctor. I have patients to see. I must get back to the pathology department of the hospital. I'm late due to my accident yesterday, so I'll have to work late." She put out her hand. "It's so nice to see you again, and I hope you'll regain your normal good health."

Morrow was taken aback by the presence of Svetlana in the room. He extended his hand to shake Svetlana's, noticing that his arm looked old and withered compared to hers. He wished he were young again. He still had a lot he wanted to accomplish.

Svetlana took note of his distress. "Don't overtax yourself, Mr. Morrow. You're obviously recovering from a trauma. I hope it wasn't too serious and that your wife and family are well."

A note of concern entered her voice, for she admired this man of unwavering principle.

"All I did was choke on a piece of meat."

Laughing, Svetlana drew up a chair and sat down next to Morrow's bed. "If you ever need help, let me know."

She gave him a look of deep concern. She meant what she said.

He sat up in bed and told her, "I want to know more about Russia. I'd like to know more so that I can help our American workers. Many have no health care. Many haven't proper accident coverage from their employers. The situation is untenable."

Svetlana nodded her head and smiled. She could hardly believe what she'd heard and was entranced by this elderly man who had lost his Senate seat to her scurrilous husband, perhaps especially as it was to her husband.

She bent close to his face and said, "I'll see what I can do. I'm so sorry you lost your seat in the Senate, even if it was to my husband. The situation in Russia is just as bad."

Morrow stared at her with disbelieving eyes. How could such a compassionate doctor be married to the unprincipled man who had unseated him? And how could it be worse in Russia?

He opened his mouth to say something, but she put her finger to her lips.

"Not now. I must see my patients. It was a pleasure to meet you, Mr. Morrow."

Svetlana stood up, straightened her Prada pants, turned a shapely leg, and left with an elegant toss of her well-coiffed head. She was what Ellie called someone who had all the luck: brains and beauty.

"Most of them don't have my Black blood," she always added, raising her chin in pride.

The two men stared at each other in surprise.

"Jameson took your Senate seat from you?"

Morrow looked down at the floor. "I'm afraid so."

"I consider him an imbecile."

"So do I," said Morrow, shifting his weight and getting up on unsteady feet to use the bathroom. "The workers are already losing many of the benefits I fought long and hard for. But then I was a miner before I became a senator, as was my poor father before me."

Boris watched him totter toward the bathroom and tried to collect his thoughts. This was a bit much even for a Russian spy. He'd thought Morrow could help him gain access to what went on behind closed doors in the Senate and to just how prepared the USA was to deter a Soviet missile, but he realized Morrow no longer had access to those closed rooms full of secret information. He hoped that he had friends who did.

Boris smiled his best crocodile smile when Morrow reappeared from the bathroom.

"How would you like to visit Moscow?" he asked rather bluntly.

Morrow's eyes squinted in Boris's direction. "What an interesting idea."

Just then, the older doctor entered the room, dressed in his white coat with, of course, a stethoscope.

"I'm going to examine you. The phlebotomist will come in for a blood draw shortly." He checked their vitals and listened to their hearts with concern. "You look like you're doing much better." He took out his stethoscope and put it under Morrow's gown. "I'd like you to take a stress test in order to make sure your heart is okay." Then he turned his attention to Boris. "Let me have a look at that head wound."

Boris grimaced. Doctor Mandel closed the curtain that divided the two beds and started to unwrap and clean the wound.

"You were lucky. It's just a superficial wound."

He cleaned it and put a new bandage on it.

"When can I leave the hospital?"

"That depends on the blood tests. You've had head trauma, so we have to make sure there are no underlying injuries. I've ordered another CT scan of your brain."

The doctor put his stethoscope on Boris's heart to be on the side of caution. Boris squirmed under the cold metal.

Morrow listened intently from his bed. He smelled a rat. Perhaps he should invite him to dinner to find out more about Russia.

Chapter 4

Bill Jameson had had several gin and tonics at the Gridiron Club with his crony Jack Smith from the Population Control Committee. His hair was mussed, and his shirt rumpled from playing a little poker. He stretched like a big bear waking from hibernation and stood up.

"Gotta go back to the missus." He gave a sloppy wink to his buddy.

He staggered a bit; his friend joined him. They were both drunk as skunks.

"Come on, Senator! We've got options up the ying-yang." He elbowed Jameson in the ribs.

Jameson laughed. "Yeah. Tell me! The Market's closed. What options?"

His friend grabbed his glass of gin from the leather-topped table at the elegant Gridiron Club. He glanced at one of the Venetian chandeliers, rubbing his red-streaked eyes.

"The girls." His eyes glazed over.

Jameson turned and faced him with a sloppy grin. "Yeah? I like girls!"

"How old?"

"No preference, just so they're pretty…and I like big tits."

Jack Smith feigned shock. "Big what? Bill, is that a way to talk?"

"You asked."

They guffawed as they walked unsteadily out of the exclusive club. A few of the other well-heeled clients turned their heads and smiled. The waiters gave each other knowing looks.

"Just follow me. I know what you want and how to get it…Um, how're ya fixed for cash?"

"I've got a few hundreds on me…ya know…for emergencies."

An elegant Black doorman opened the heavy mahogany door carved with lions. "Do you gentlemen need assistance?"

"Don't worry 'bout us, Jamal," said Smith, pushing some cash in his hand.

"I think I should call a cab, Sir."

Smith gave him a dirty look. "Ya think we're drunk, don't ya? Well, we just have leg cramps from sitting and writing environmental bills all day." Unable to control his laughter, he doubled over, nearly falling.

The doorman whistled, "Taxi!"

A cab pulled up in front of the carpet that led to the club. The doorman helped the men get in.

"What about my car?" said Jameson, slurring his words.

"Shut up and get ready to have some fun," said Smith. "17176 Georgetown Road, driver!"

The driver nodded, pulled his bright-yellow taxi from the curb, and headed to Georgetown.

They arrived in fifteen minutes. The area was classic Georgetown with elegant narrow two-story brick buildings with turn-of-the-century detailed stairways and doors. It was a lovely evening with a crescent moon.

The driver parked and got out to assist the two drunken men. They giggled like schoolboys as they got out of the cab.

The driver scowled when they left him a dollar tip. "Cheap bastards! And they take our pensions away with their crummy bills!"

An expensively dressed woman of about fifty wearing an especially low-cut dress with lots of sequins, with her hair piled high on her head, opened the door of 17176 Georgetown Road to see what the cat had dragged in. She spotted Jack Smith and grinned. She could taste the money already. She ran to greet them.

"What an honor to have such distinguished gentlemen pay us a visit," she trilled in a falsetto voice.

Smith made a clumsy bow, almost falling on his face as the cab pulled away.

"The honor is all ours, Maggie! Why, I haven't seen you in—"

"A week! Far too long," she squealed. "And who is the elegant gentleman you've brought with you?"

"Him? He's Billy Boy, a new guy. You'll have to give him the TLC treatment." He tripped on the rug and nearly fell down but straightened up as Jameson looked on, still drunk. "He can sing too!"

Jameson blanched and wondered if Smith was referring to his embarrassing faux pas in front of the entire Senate when he broke into song for no reason. He jerked his head around, only to see Smith playing with the madam's pearls.

"Yeah, TLC is what we want!"

"Then come on in," said Maggie, hoisting her skirt so she wouldn't trip as she walked up the stairs to a doorway.

She took Smith's hand off her bodice, putting her arm through his to make sure he didn't take a tumble. Jameson held onto the wrought-iron railing and started laughing for no reason.

Smith cupped his hand to his mouth. "That guy has had a few too many."

"Nah! He's just out on the town. Come on in, fellas!"

Maggie opened the door to a sumptuous room decorated with velvet curtains drawn shut, dimly lit chandeliers and, Louis XVI furniture covered in velvet.

"Lafayette left us the furniture," tittered Maggie.

Ten or so young women, some not more than sixteen years old, of all racial backgrounds adorned the furniture, wearing sexy late-teen dresses which showed off their breasts and legs.

Jameson's eyes grew wider as he surveyed the room and the girls. "Hi!" He waved in their direction.

The girls eyed him. "Hi, Daddy," they chorused without a lot of enthusiasm.

They exchanged looks, knowing what was in store for one of them.

Maggie gave them a mean look. "You can do better than that!"

They stood and swiveled their hips. "Hello, handsome gentlemen," they trilled as if they meant it.

Jameson sat down with a thud on a green velvet-covered Louis XV chair. Smith and Maggie laughed at him. Maggie signaled to one of the Black girls, who walked over and sat daintily on his lap. She was tall and stiletto thin with a lovely smile.

Jameson stared at her well-shaped breasts under a very filmy camisole and sucked in his breath. He'd always wanted to have sex with a Black girl. He kissed her on the cheek.

"I see you like me," said the girl.

"Yeah. You know what they say. The more you drink, the better they look." He laughed at his insulting joke, which amused only him.

Khadija lifted an eyebrow. He was business, and she needed business. So she forced herself to smile. She could smell his rank sweat mixed with alcohol. She detested him.

"Let's dance!" She grabbed him by the waist and started waltzing him around the carpeted floor, trying to tire him out.

Drunk, he stumbled now and then. She did her best to hold him up. Maggie put on "The Blue Danube." She shot a sly look at Smith, who shrugged.

"Guess he knows what he wants."

"It's gonna cost ya. You know the rules." Maggie gave Jack Smith a sly look.

He handed her a couple of hundred dollars, laughed, and then walked over to Jameson.

"Hey, where's the cash?"

Jameson stopped dancing. "Cash? Huh? What for?"

"A middle-aged man doesn't get to dance with a girl this pretty for free."

Jameson shook his head, insulted. "I'm not middle aged!"

He sucked in his stomach in an attempt to look svelte.

"The cash, buddy, the cash."

Drawing his breath in a deep sigh, Jameson fished in his wallet for some cash. "At least it's free with Sveta."

"Shut up, fool. We don't talk about our wives in here!" Smith slapped him on the back hard. *Shouldn't have given him that vial.* "He's a little punchy tonight, but once you get to know him, you'll love him! Why, he built the Jameson Towers!"

"The Jameson Towers!" repeated the girls in mock admiration. "He's really rich!"

"Yeah, so treat him right."

The girl he'd been dancing with twirled him around a couple of times, laughing. Jameson looked at her in surprise. "Why, aren't you something else!" He spotted the spiral staircase. "Where's that lead to?"

"A lot more cash." Smith winked, feeling like a stud with a few whiskeys under his belt. "Shut up and have some fun!"

Khadija turned to look for another girl. None was forthcoming. "Will you be my sugar daddy?" she asked coyly, resolving to make it a quick one.

"Honey, I'll be whatever you want me to be!" Jameson took her hand and pulled her toward the staircase.

Maggie stepped in between Jameson and the staircase, her hand outstretched. Jameson scratched his head. He handed her the rest of his cash as he and the young lady climbed the magical staircase to underage sex.

Once they arrived at the door of her suite, which was decorated in hearts and kissy lips, she turned and asked, "Do you mind telling me your name, sir?"

Jameson cleared his throat. "Ah, John," he managed to sputter through his alcoholic daze.

She laughed. "Oh, how original! Well, I'm Khadija."

"Huh?" mumbled Jameson as he surveyed the gilt-trimmed room and Khadija's breasts.

His cell phone rang. He took it out of the pocket in his trousers, silencing it with a guilty grin. He put it in his jacket pocket.

"Was that your grandma?"

He stared soddenly at Khadija, who drew him toward a sumptuous Louis XVI canopy bed with silken sheets. She gave him a gentle push. He landed on the bed with a soft thud.

"My grandmother? Yeah, she calls me all the time. Loves me. This is some bed you've got here."

"Yes, it's really comfy." Khadija grinned, pushing him toward the center.

Jameson lay down and started snoring immediately. Khadija removed his jacket and inspected his wallet. She saw that he was

Senator William Jameson from West Virginia. She examined his gold-embossed card from the US Senate and smiled, thinking that she may have caught a big fish.

I'll bet he votes against abortion and then gives us money to get one, she thought. *And that phone call...must've been his sweet little wife. Maybe I can make enough money to go to college. If I play my cards right, I can get into Harvard...and help my sister.*

She snuggled up against his limp form and fell asleep, hoping he wouldn't rape her in the morning.

Jameson farted and tugged at the bed covers, leaving her with little more than her sexy Gucci party dress for a blanket. She sighed, getting up to drag a warm coat to throw over herself for the duration of the night.

Jameson tossed and turned during the night. He dreamed that Morrow was shaking his finger at him for his indiscretion. He snorted at him and started to sing "Mary Had a Little Lamb" like he did in the Senate. He threw something at Morrow in his dream, who yelled something to the effect that he was a bottom-feeder. Jameson started screaming at him. His screams awakened Khadija, who recoiled. She examined the distraught man next to her, ready to run into the hall. She stroked his head instead, which calmed him, and he fell into a deep sleep, snoring. She breathed a sigh of relief. Another annoying one. She managed to fall asleep despite the disgusting swine next to her. A tiny red light blinked from the hidden camera that recorded their movements.

Morning dawned soon enough. Bright rays of Georgetown sunshine lit up the haute decor room. Jameson grunted, cleared his throat, and rolled over on Khadija wrapped in her plaid wool coat. Only someone with dark skin and a razor-thin figure could wear it and look as good as she did although she wasn't at her best at 6:00 a.m.

"Hey!" she yelled.

Jameson shook himself awake, unsure of where he was and with whom. "Where am I?"

"Don't you remember...John?" Khadija looked at him and grinned a sweet, toothy grin, a teenage grin.

She sat up in bed and put on her slippers. *Drunken senator* ran through her mind.

"I have to go."

Jameson grabbed her by the arm and heaved his heavy body onto her small one. It was over in two minutes, during which she resolved never to see him again. She didn't care if he were the king of Siam. The red light went off.

Maybe I won't have to, she thought as she pushed him off her, scurrying to the bathroom like the frightened kid she was.

Jameson remembered some of his drunken evening, concluding that his friend had left him in this mantrap. He quickly turned on his cell phone and punched his assistant's name. She didn't answer, so he left a message saying that he might come to the Senate at around noon. Then he listened to the voice message from his wife.

"Accident. Not seriously injured. Please come to the Columbus Hospital."

Shocked into reality, he stood up, straightened his rumpled clothes, tightened his tie, and ran his fingers through his golden locks. A look of apprehension came over his face as he checked for his wallet in his pants pocket. He breathed a deep sigh of relief that it was there.

Hoping this man wasn't going to ask her to do anything other than leave, she tried to smile at him, but all she could do was grimace.

"May I?"

"Most certainly, John," she replied, holding her breath.

He noted her beautiful skin, large dark eyes, and slim figure and took a deep breath. He pulled her to him and kissed her, feeling her nubile breasts.

"Thank you, Miss…"

"Khadija," she snarled.

"Ah, how could I forget such a lovely name…such a lovely girl. Thank you."

He whisked into the bathroom to call the hospital to see if they could page Svetlana. The nurse on duty told him she'd be there by nine.

What a woman, he thought, wondering how in the hell they'd gotten together.

That night at the Russian embassy, she looked so beautiful in the moonlight on the balustrade.

His mind wandered. *Morrow. I dreamed of that little rat.*

Jameson looked perplexed. He had gotten involved in more than he could handle. He shook his head, wondering what they had come up with at Fort Bener. Odious thoughts filled his mind as he remembered granting them permission to experiment on people.

*Svetlana's patient…*He shrugged.

He knew people did horrible things to one another. The image of his great-great-grandfather raping a slave on their old plantation in what was once Virginia flashed before his eyes. He shook his head again, thinking of Khadija. It was too much for him to contemplate all at once. He'd repressed all those old plantation stories. That people voted to split the beautiful state of Virginia into separate states, West Virginia being the antislavery state, still rankled.

He vanished into the bathroom, where he jumped into a convenient shower. As he scrubbed his armpit, he wished he had clean underwear. He'd give anything for clean underwear.

I'll have to rough it today, he thought to himself. *And what about Khadija? Svetlana, accident…*His foggy, hungover mind stalled.

Morrow kept coming into his thoughts. It was all he could do to dry off, dress, and stumble back into the velour-coated room with… that girl. He wondered how old she might have been. Excuses to leave ran through his mind. Khadija was prepared for him. She'd seen that the hidden camera was still recording their interactions. She giggled.

"What's so funny?"

A coy look was all she could manage. "Why, you, of course. Getting up and showering so bright and early. You must be a very successful businessman."

Jameson was already edging toward the door. He asked her, "Do I owe…"

"Please! We don't talk about such things here." She turned her back to him, which looked very tempting with her nice little round bottom, but now was not the time.

"Of course not…Haj…"

"Khadija."

"Of course not, Khadija. It was a pleasure meeting you." He kissed her on the neck.

She turned away fast, giggling. "Oh, you big sexy thing. That tickles!"

"Thank you for…" Jameson was at a loss for words.

"The pleasure was all mine," she cooed.

Jameson looked at her face as she examined his. They locked eyes for about thirty seconds. He was transfixed. She was mysterious. The crucifix around her neck made her even more tempting.

A foster kid whose parents weren't exactly ideal, she'd ended up on the streets. Maggie's place had seemed like a haven after what she'd been through with her foster father. But she knew she was smart because she was still in school at Washington and Lee High and doing well. She even aced her last geometry exam. She knew right angles and all the rest like the palm of her hand. She did homework whenever she had a spare minute.

She stared at Jameson as he started to take off his coat again. He jumped her like a true oaf and tore her clothes off.

"Careful with the Gucci dress!" she yelled as they went down.

After five minutes of wild sex, he came. Khadija breathed a sigh of relief.

Thank goodness for the birth control pill ran through her turbulent seventeen-year-old mind.

Jameson grabbed his pants and dressed in a flash.

After all, I have to get my money's worth went through his mind as he turned toward the door.

"I must go now." He gasped, opening the door and racing for the front door, where a groggy doorman stopped him.

"You leaving us so soon?"

"I have an important engagement."

"Yes, they all do. Did you enjoy your night with Khadija?"

Jameson was thrown off guard. How did this kid know where he'd slept and with whom?

"It was very restful. Maybe I'll come again in a few weeks."

Khadija, who listened from the doorway, narrowed her eyes and yelled, "Don't bother! You're horrible in bed."

Jameson's bleary eyes all but popped out of his head. He slapped her in the face. She slapped him back. They went down, yelling as they pummeled each other. Maggie stepped in and blew a whistle. The doorman yanked Jameson off a panting Khadija, stood him on his two feet, and pushed him out the door. Khadija leaned against the wall, sliding slowly to the floor. She put her face in her hands.

"JERK!"

Jameson's face turned beet red. "Whore!"

Khadija laughed. "As if I have a choice."

"Of course, you'll leave a gratuity for our hospitality," said the young doorman, quite proficient in extracting money from these horny dudes as he pushed him down the brick stairs.

Jameson fished through his pockets, vaguely remembering Smith and the woman and cash and being very drunk. He fingered a couple of twenties.

"For your…college education," he said with a turn of his shoulder so that he wouldn't be recognized.

He had to get out of there. And where was Smith?

The doorman snaked the twenties out of his hand so fast that he realized he was not dealing with a novice.

"Say goodbye to the lady of the house for me." He turned and started to look for a cab.

"Yes, of course, Mr.?"

"Mr.?" A sly smile glazed Jameson's face. "Mr. Morrow. Walter Morrow."

"Thank you, Mr. Morrow. And have a nice day." He tipped his doorman's cap and hailed a taxi. "Taxi! Taxi!" he yelled.

A cabby pulled up next to Jameson, giving the doorman a knowing wink. Jameson jumped in the back seat, fishing for his iPhone in his suit pockets, wondering what had happened to his wife.

"To the…United States Post Office on Fifth Avenue!"

"Sure, buddy. But you don't look like no mailman to me."

"I'm in the administration."

"Yeah. Okay."

Jameson left Svetlana a message saying that he hoped she was all right. It was too much for him to deal with: the drunken night in a brothel, his wife in an accident, and especially the dream about his nemesis, Walter Morrow. He had to render him harmless.

Perhaps an injection, his mind fogged over.

The post office was close enough to the Capitol Building that he could walk while calling Svetlana again to see about her accident. He breathed deeply, relieved not to have been seen coming out of that house—that house Smith took him to as a joke.

It must have been a prank, he thought with irritation.

The image of Khadija's sweet smiling face and taut round bottom ran through his consciousness. Profanity ran through his mind.

She said I was bad in bed. What a nerve.

Back at the Georgetown hotel, Maggie checked her computer for footage of Khadija's and Jameson's night of pleasure. Khadija slipped past her to go to the nearby Catholic church and confess her sins to the priest. She was devout.

Chapter 5

Boris walked out of the hospital, wondering what to do next. He'd messed up his KGB assignment to kill Svetlana, so he knew he'd be fired or worse. A keen desire to see his Russian wife and children coursed through his brain. They'd have their eyes on his family too, he realized, but perhaps he could hide in plain sight.

What a fantasy, he chided himself. *There's no way that I can safely return to Russia.*

He walked down the wintry street, clutching his long wool coat around him and feeling a sharp stab of pain from his head wound. It reminded him of the hospital—of that strange man in the bed next to him. Mr. Morrow. Mr. Walter Morrow. He had said that he wanted to go to Russia and had a bizarre fascination with the working class.

Where did he say he lived?

Boris's mind fogged over. He felt dizzy. He was at the end of his rope. He sat down on a bench. It was cold, and he began to shiver. Gray clouds announced a downpour. Rain began to splatter on him. He had to get home, if you could call the room he rented a home. Morrow had said he was from West Virginia. How could he arrange a trip to Russia for him? He could say he was his tour guide. Random thoughts ran through his turgid mind. Desperation had set in.

He dialed information on his cell phone and asked for Walter Morrow of West Virginia. The operator gave him a number.

This is too easy. It won't work, he thought, but he dialed the number anyway.

Ellie Morrow answered.

"Could I speak to Mr. Walter Morrow? He's not to be disturbed right now? Could I leave my number? Yes, of course."

Boris gave Ellie his cell phone number. He took a deep breath and started thinking of ways to raise enough money to fly to Russia. He knew he couldn't ask his superiors, after botching his assignment to kill Svetlana, without perhaps lethal punishment. Lacking the money to fly to parts unknown and hide, he began to tremble. Maybe he could talk the treasurer into extending some extra funds for a trip to Moscow with a former US senator who had Communist sympathies, perhaps taking the former senator hostage. His mind blurred. Nothing made much sense today.

His cell phone beeped. Morrow was on the line.

"Could you come to West Virginia for dinner with me and my family?"

Morrow's voice was throaty and hard to understand from having to eject that piece of meat that got stuck in his windpipe. He cleared his throat.

"I'd love to have dinner with you and your family," purred Boris.

He couldn't believe his luck. This man was the perfect tool for the KGB. He wrote down the date for the dinner and started to walk at a brisk pace. Things were falling into place. The rain felt good on his tired face.

In his home in West Virginia, Walter Morrow ran his fingers through his thick white hair, wondering if he'd invited the fox into the henhouse. He shook his head to clear his thoughts.

"He's such a nice man," he said to his wife, who smiled gamely. "You're going to like him, Ellie!"

"What if he's a spy?" Ellie laughed, trying to make light of the dinner invitation.

"I hope he can give us some insight into Mother Russia," said Morrow.

"I've never met a Russian before. Wonder what they're doing to stop child trafficking?" She smiled at her sweet husband, whom she loved for his big heart.

Still, she'd watch this Russian with an eagle eye. Ellie was the iron maiden of the family although everyone thought she was an angel.

Chapter 6

Svetlana woke up alone in bed at home. For the first time, her husband had stayed out all night, a night when she most needed his help. After convincing the police that the gunshot was an accident, she took a taxi to the hospital. She caught a ride home with a colleague. Her car was totaled. She'd call the insurance company and get a rental until they could give her the money to buy a new one, for this one looked like it was beyond repair: a smashed front end and bullet holes in the dashboard. As for Bill Jameson, she suspected he was dallying; so perhaps she'd have to divorce him or, better yet, to do something more devious. She'd learned a lot of tricks as a Soviet spy.

She got up fast and went to the closet where she'd hidden a gun. She took it and went through the house with it pointed in front of her, using both arms to swing the Glock around from time to time to make sure no one was behind her. She knew she would be followed after her run-in with Boris. Her life had changed overnight, but she was used to this. She ate a hurried breakfast, then she ran to her closet, feeling through it to make sure no one was hiding there. Donning a dress and her hospital whites, she called ahead to let them know she'd had an accident last night but would be there as soon as the taxi could traverse the Beltway.

She watched the monuments honoring liberty and its heroes as the taxi cruised down the Beltway—the Lincoln Memorial, the Washington Memorial, and finally the Jefferson Memorial—as the cab crossed the magnificent granite bridge that led to Columbus Hospital. Saying a silent prayer that these monuments to freedom would watch over her, she paid the cab driver and rushed to the department of toxicology.

"Are you sure you're all right?" asked the receptionist, her brown ponytail bobbing as she stood up.

Svetlana smiled her professional smile. "It was just a minor scrape."

Next, she saw her colleague's nurse, June Johnson, a petite Black woman with carefully coiffed hair.

"Dr. Elder would like to talk to you," she murmured as Svetlana swept into her office, where papers, patients' exam results, and lab orders were piled high.

"I'd like to see him too," she nearly shouted over her shoulder.

The waiting workload, plus the autopsy results of the patient who had died of unknown causes, awaited her; she knew she had a tough day ahead. She dove into the papers with alacrity.

"Where is Mr. Svetlensky's autopsy report?"

Her assistant delved into the pile of results and came up with the autopsy marked in red.

Svetlana nodded and took it, reading fast. "Creatinine abnormal. Liver hardened. Unknown toxins found. Further analysis is necessary." Svetlana picked up the hospital phone and clicked on the autopsy lab. "Hello? We must continue the assessment of Mr. Svetlensky. Look for all known poisons," she said.

"Yes, Dr. Jameson," replied the toxicologist working in the autopsy lab. "We're working on it. We've tested for anthrax, strychnine, and—"

"It may be something you haven't seen before. Could you call London to find out how to trace the toxins used on the Russian agent?"

Svetlana heard the toxicologist hesitate.

"Um, yes, which hospital was he in?"

"London General Hospital," said Svetlana.

She'd followed the case closely in the newspapers. She also realized that the British Defense Science and Technology Laboratory had all the details.

"Yes, Dr. Jameson, right away."

Svetlana hung up the phone and busied herself with calling in orders. She was examining a patient when her husband walked in. The patient was wearing a hospital gown while Svetlana put her stethoscope to her heart.

"You can't walk in while I'm examining a patient!" She took the stethoscope off the patient and whirled around angrily.

"I just did." He walked toward her.

"Get out, or I'll call security!" She looked for a scalpel or any sharp-edged instrument to use to defend herself. "You look terrible and should be in Congress!"

The patient's eyes widened.

Svetlana turned to her. "I'm sorry for this unforgivable breach of hospital etiquette! We'll discuss last night at home, Bill!" She walked to her desk and eyed the security button.

Jameson grabbed her wrist. "What makes you think I'm coming home tonight?"

She gave him a furious look. "What are you doing?"

"Working late and sleeping in the office. It's tough, but I'm a senator, and it's my duty to American citizens. Did you say you wanted your daughter to immigrate?" He let go of her wrist with a twist.

"Leave!" Svetlana scowled, furious that he had alluded to Nadia, her daughter.

He laughed at her. "On second thought, I will come home tonight. I will expect a New York steak for dinner." He walked out of the door and into the reception area with an arrogant flourish of his arm.

Svetlana turned to her patient. "This is highly irregular. I apologize."

Her elderly white-haired patient had a bemused look on her face. "Don't worry. I wish you luck with your husband." She pursed her lips. "I've been married twice. It can be trying."

Svetlana looked into the woman's wizened, wrinkled face that had once been beautiful. "I'll follow your lab results with utmost attention."

"As you do all your patients' lab results."

This time, Svetlana's eyes widened. "Of course," she said and nodded her head in deference to the elderly woman's perspicacity.

Svetlana ducked out the door so that her patient could dress in privacy.

She strode to the reception desk of toxicology. The receptionist looked up, awaiting her orders.

"Have you received the results of the autopsy I ordered yesterday?"

A hefty blond with her hair done up in a French twist cleared her throat. "Ah, they should be here. Haven't they shown up on your computer?"

"They're top secret. I asked them to send them to me directly, not on a computer which can be hacked."

"Of course!" The receptionist turned and looked at a pile of papers. She swiveled her chair and laughed. "They must be here somewhere. I'll let you know as soon as I find them."

Svetlana took off her glasses and tapped her foot. "Never mind. I'll call the coroner."

"But they must be here!" The receptionist fumbled through the pile of papers.

"I'm sure they are, but I'll call to make sure. Thank you." She turned, running full tilt to her office, where she picked up the inter-office phone. "Hello, this is Dr. Svetlana Jameson. Could you give me the results of the autopsy I requested?" She fiddled nervously with a paper on her desk, trying to read and talk at the same time.

The coroner blinked rapidly as he spoke to Svetlana. "The results are negative. No cause of death could be determined." He took a deep breath and looked at the door leading to the morgue.

"What? He had to die of something!"

"Yes, I know, but we couldn't determine the cause. We ran the tests for poisonings that you suggested and did the regular autopsy as well."

The rail-thin dark-haired head of the autopsy ward stood up and began to pace the floor. Svetlana made him nervous.

These female doctors are so demanding, he thought.

"I'll come to examine the body during my lunch hour."

"Yes, Doctor Jameson," he replied with a nervous flick of his tongue. *She's going to be thorough*, he thought, annoyed.

That meant more work for him, and he was already deluged.

"We'll have the body waiting for you."

"Thank you kindly," said Svetlana with a trace of a smile on her lips. A waiting corpse. Who did they think she was, Dracula?

Bodies lay covered in a heavy black tarp in the morgue. Svetlana walked up to one of them and examined its skin color.

"This looks like some sort of poisoning," she said to the anxious coroner, who followed her with mincing steps.

"It's possible. We can't trace everything since they've developed new poisons, some of which are untraceable, unfortunately."

He took out a handkerchief and mopped his perspiring brow as he examined Svetlana's well-turned ankles and shapely calves.

This woman is too beautiful to be a doctor ran through his fevered brain.

"Do you mind if I try to trace something?"

She turned and gave him her best professional smile, which was almost too much for the perspiring coroner. He never knew how to talk to women of this caliber.

"Yes, yes, do whatever you like." He rubbed his hands nervously on his white coroner's jacket.

"Thank you. If you don't mind, I'll proceed immediately."

He nodded and withdrew, walking backward as if in the presence of royalty.

Svetlana smiled a broad smile, realizing the poor man was intimidated by her. When he shut the door, she turned; donned a pair of coroner's gloves, extra thick; and examined the eyes, which had yellow pupils, a sign of jaundice and poisoning, perhaps of slow onset. She bowed her head in thought, trying to summon to mind similar cases. She remembered a victim of the KGB killed by microwave poisoning. Tears came to her eyes; it had been a friend of hers, ordered eliminated by her superiors. She repressed memories of her late husband's even more tragic demise.

Breathing deeply to steady herself, she took a vial out of one of the pockets of her doctor's smock and made an incision with a tiny scalpel into the corpse's inner ear in order to withdraw some brain gray matter. She looked at the vial with satisfaction and pocketed it.

She leaned against a table with another corpse laid out on it and accidentally felt its chest. It was a woman. She gasped, then ran hurriedly out of the morgue. She hoped she'd never end up in a morgue with a doctor poking at her brain.

I need a healthy lunch and some time to think, time to regain my sanity.

Thoughts of the KGB plagued her. Memories of her Russian husband and her daughter surged through her brain; she could no longer repress them. Tears began to well up in her eyes. She wiped them away with the cuff of her white doctor's coat and broke into a run.

It was cold and windy outside. She pulled on a woolen coat and shivered as she ran, the wind raking her hair. It felt good to have wind in her hair. She breathed deeply and did the mental exercises she had learned in order to keep these images from turning her into a distraught, crying woman who would be of no use to anyone.

She saw a small restaurant and went in. A waitress nodded toward the red-checkered table in the corner, and Svetlana sat down at it. She put her head in her hands in despair. She took a deep breath, shook her head, and straightened up. The vision of her first husband wouldn't leave her mind. The revolver the KGB agent pointed at his head had blurred her vision. She breathed deeply again.

Noticing her distress, the waitress asked, "Do you want me to come back later, Doctor?"

Svetlana shook her head. "No, I have to eat and get back to the hospital. I'm just...just having a bad moment...It will pass..."

"Would you like a glass of water?"

Svetlana nodded her head. "Please. And a hamburger or a tuna fish sandwich."

"We have hamburgers." The waitress scribbled hamburger on her pad and walked away, shaking her head in sympathy.

Svetlana took a deep breath. She knew she had to blot out the memory of the day that her husband was killed, or she wouldn't be able to finish her heavy schedule at the hospital. Others needed help. She had to fulfill her obligation as a physician. Random thoughts ran through her head like a freight train, her blonde hair now mussed from running down the windy street.

That snowy, wintry evening in Moscow chilled her to the bone; she prepared a hasty dinner with her daughter sitting at the kitchen table, doing her math homework. The knock on the door came as a surprise. Her almost impossibly good-looking husband stood up from where he'd been reading a document with a fairly bland look on his face. She remembered it well, the blood gushing from his gunshot wound. Her head started to spin. She pinched both her cheeks to keep from fainting.

The waitress, a hefty blond woman, walked to her table and placed a hamburger with a bottle of Heinz ketchup in front of her. Svetlana peered into her eyes as if searching for a life preserver. She couldn't bear up another minute.

The waitress felt her intense stare and flinched. "Are you okay, sweetie?"

Svetlana shook her head to try to compose herself. "Yes, thank you for asking. I'm just hungry." She smiled at the waitress as best she could.

The waitress nodded with a look of uncertainty. "Eat hearty." She grinned, trying to seem cheerful.

"Thanks," said Svetlana.

She began to wolf down the hamburger as if she hadn't eaten in days, which reminded her of her flight out of Russia with the hounds of hell at her heels. She forced herself to eat. The taste of hamburger and ketchup brought her back to reality although thoughts kept bouncing through her head.

Boris will be after me, she realized. *I've got to get out while I can... Who can help me?*

The visage of the elderly senator that her husband had defeated came to her mind for some reason. Little did she know he had invited Boris to dinner.

Back at the hospital, after taking the vial of brain tissue to pathology for analysis of rare autoimmune system poisons, she looked up Mr. Morrow's name and address, picked up her phone, and called his home.

Ellie answered. "Hello, Senator Walter Morrow's residence."

Svetlana arched her brow and stifled a laugh at the reference to Morrow as a senator even though he'd been defeated. It must have been hard on him.

"This is Dr. Svetlana Jameson. I saw Mr., um, Senator Morrow in the hospital. Could I speak to him?"

"Yes, of course. I'm sure he'd like to talk to you, Dr. Jameson."

Morrow looked up from the easy chair, where he was perusing the latest news, all bad. Deep cuts had been made into working people's pensions and health care. He felt his heart race. He stood up and walked over to take the call.

"Hello, this is Walter Morrow. Are you a miner?" He laughed. "I talk to other people too."

Svetlana smiled, a man after her own heart. He had a sense of humor, something she sorely missed after the KGB had killed her husband, who had been so full of life and laughter. And love. So much love.

"This is just one of the doctors who looked in on you during your hospitalization, Mr. Morrow. My name is Svetlana Jameson."

"Jameson? I know that name!" Morrow walked back to his chair, the phone held to his ear.

"It must be strange to receive a call from Senator Jameson's wife, but this is somewhat urgent. A patient has died of an unknown poison, and I need to get in touch with someone who cares about, shall we say, the little people?"

"I care about them. I was one of them before I was elected to the Senate. But wouldn't your husband object to your speaking with me?" Mr. Morrow settled into his easy chair.

"We're going to divorce. I hate to drag personal matters into this, but I'm Russian, and I heard that you were interested in helping the working class. I'd love to talk to you. Perhaps I can help."

"How can you help?" Morrow frowned, wondering what made these Russians tick.

Svetlana took off one of her shoes and leaned against the desk to be more comfortable. "I think I can help you regain your seat in the Senate."

Morrow sat up straight in surprise. Ellie widened her eyes.

"He's been comporting himself in a very undignified manner with his colleagues and with women. I have videos. He might even have access to nerve poison."

Morrow's eyes widened and met Ellie's. "He has?"

"Could we meet to discuss it?"

Two nurses walked by and looked at Svetlana leaning against the desk, talking passionately on the phone. She ignored them. They nodded at her in deference. She didn't notice.

"I…I don't know what to say," stammered Morrow. "Could you give me your number? Let me think it over. I'm just a simple man, a man of the people, but I'm a helluva fighter. I fight for ordinary people's rights." Morrow stood up and put his arm around his wife. "We're regular folk, and my serving in the Senate didn't change us."

"Good! Call me at your convenience. I hope I haven't upset you in any way, Mr. …um, Senator Morrow. I feel that you and the American people have been cheated. I want to set things right. So much that is demeaning is going on in your Senate…"

She put her shoe back on and straightened her spine, ready to resume examining patients.

"Yes, that's true. I'll call you tomorrow. I'll have to talk this over with my wife."

Ellie smiled at her husband and squeezed his shoulder. They beamed at one another.

"Quite right. One should never act in haste. Thank you for your consideration, Senator Morrow."

Svetlana had to click off the phone. A doctor was approaching her at a rapid pace.

Walter and Ellie Morrow looked at each other in mild shock.

"What a world we live in," she murmured.

He hugged her tight.

"Didn't you invite her husband to dinner?"

Walter slaps his forehead. "By gum, I did. What got into me?"

Ellie hugged him tighter, hoping things would turn out for the best.

Chapter 7

Svetlana pulled into the driveway of her elegant colonial brick house and pressed the garage door opener. It opened, and she parked the car. She got out, looking around, making sure that no one was watching. She walked to the door and unlocked it. She opened the door to her home and listened. Her husband hadn't come home. Breathing a deep sigh of relief, she kicked off her high heels. She sat down on the sofa and read the *Washington Post*, but thoughts of her husband's dalliance kept running through her head.

"That soulless fool," she muttered, standing up and walking to the kitchen.

She opened some cupboards and the refrigerator, taking out some beets to prepare borscht for dinner. It was her favorite food. She knew Americans didn't like it very much, especially Jameson, the esteemed senator and her wayward hubby.

She was stirring the soup when the door opened, and he appeared, his face drawn and weary. She almost felt sorry for him. He was carrying something in a bag.

"Hi, Sveta." He gave her a peck on the cheek and then headed for the bathroom.

Svetlana turned and said, "You look exhausted. Where have you been?"

She heard the bathroom door slam shut.

Jameson opened the bag in the bathroom and hid the contents behind some cotton balls in the medicine chest. He had talked Smith into giving him vials of anthrax from Fort Bener after threatening to reveal his activities at Maggie's brothel. Then he turned on the shower, undressed, and got in, taking his time.

Svetlana stirred the borscht, inhaling the acrid aroma of beets that took her back to Moscow.

"If only I could go home," she murmured to herself.

Then she laughed at the absurdity of her situation, a Jewish Russian former spy whose first husband had been assassinated. She knew she had to steer clear of Russia and its secret service.

The landline phone rang. She put the soup spoon on a ladle and walked over to the phone.

"Hello."

Walter Morrow hesitated for a second or two. "Is this the residence of Senator Jameson?"

"Yes, it is. Who's calling, please?" Svetlana sat down in the armchair next to the phone and loosened her luxuriant long hair.

"Um, this is Mr. Walter Morrow. Is this Dr. Jameson?"

"Yes." Her voice filled with expectancy.

She crossed her legs and smiled, sensing the possibility.

"My wife, Ellie, and I would like to invite you to dinner to discuss…um, matters."

Morrow hemmed and hawed, feeling embarrassed delving into another person's private life. He scratched his head, avoiding the small bald spot on top.

Ellie stared at him, wondering how she might help her husband.

"My husband is in the shower right now. Give me your address, please."

"I wanted to invite you and Boris, the other patient who is also Russian, to my house for dinner to discuss workers' rights. It's very important."

Svetlana frowned at the mention of Boris's name. "I'm the one you should talk to, Mr. Morrow. I care about workers' rights. Boris… and my husband…don't."

Morrow shook his head in disbelief. "But he told me he did. I'm sure you care about people's rights as well. We can discuss your husband's…motives another time."

Svetlana stood up and looked at the borscht, which was boiling over.

"Why don't you invite me first? Perhaps I can help you understand both Boris and my husband better."

Morrow stared at Ellie, who hunched her shoulders, not knowing what to think. He furrowed his brow, then brightened.

"That's a good idea. I don't understand him at all. You are from Russia, aren't you?"

"Yes."

Morrow plopped down on the sofa. He was nonplussed.

"So you know someone named Boris? The man who was in the hospital with me?"

Svetlana smiled. "Yes, Boris and I are old friends. But don't invite him."

"Why not?"

"Russians are funny that way. Two of us at a dinner table can be awkward." She paused. "My soup is boiling over. I must hang up. I'll be at your house tomorrow night by eight."

She put down the phone and ran to turn the flame down under the borscht.

What a *mess* ran through her head.

Walter and Ellie Morrow exchanged looks.

"Senator Jameson's wife is coming to dinner tomorrow night."

Ellie's eyes widened. "Without him?"

"She said she could explain his motives and that it would be better for her to come alone." Morrow smiled a sweet little smile at Ellie. "She said not to invite Boris at the same time because Russians…" His mind went blank.

"Anything to help the cause. Maybe she can help Adelaide's husband since she's a doctor."

Morrow took his wife by the hand and squeezed it. A tear rolled down Ellie Morrow's cheek; she couldn't help but think of Adelaide and her injured husband and so many others who were worse off.

Senator Jameson pulled on a bathrobe and walked into the kitchen. Svetlana gave him a dirty look while stirring the borscht.

He gave her a quick peck on the cheek.

"Not while I'm making borscht." Svetlana frowned at him.

He flopped onto the sofa and turned on the wide-screen plasma TV. "You Russian women are worse than American women, if that's possible!"

Svetlana started to laugh. She turned off the burner and clutched her sides.

"Worse than American women? Why don't you try an Asian wife? Maybe she'd suit you better."

Jameson shot her an angry look. "Maybe I will."

She continued to laugh, turning the borscht back on and stirring it.

"Watch what you put in that Russian concoction," he said as he changed channels, looking for a comedy to take his mind off politics.

"Would you like me to taste it first?" She started laughing again, only this time she couldn't contain herself.

Jameson got up and slapped her in the face. "Stop it!"

Sveta yelled, "Ouch!" rubbing her cheek where he hit her.

She picked up the soup and threw it at him.

He yelped as the scalding soup hit him in the chest. "You fucking bitch! I'm going to—"

He looked around and spied a knife on the wooden cutting board where Sveta had been dicing beets. He grabbed it and lunged at her. Too late. She'd already picked up the car keys and was running toward the front door. She opened it and sprinted outside, charging to the garage. Jameson was hot on her heels, but she'd already gotten in her car and was gunning the engine. She was out of the driveway before he could stop her. He flipped his middle finger at her as she drove away.

He shouted, "Cunt!" clenched his fists, and stomped back into the house, tossing the knife on the floor. *I'm going to kill that bitch.*

He punched the wall with his fist, then yelped in pain.

Boris lay in wait, his car parked in front of the house next door to spy on the Jamesons. Within half an hour of his vigil, Svetlana pulled out of the driveway and sped away.

Now I'll be able to finish her off, he thought as she sped toward the freeway.

He followed her at a discreet distance so she wouldn't spot him.

Where can I go? A thousand thoughts assailed Svetlana as she tried to think of a safe place.

Then she remembered Morrow's dinner invitation and seemingly boundless human kindness.

"They don't make them like that anymore," she murmured as she turned onto an on-ramp, driving as if the devil himself were pursuing her.

I'll go to Morrow's house in West Virginia!

She floored the gas pedal and hit ninety miles per hour. A feeling of jubilation coursed through her veins.

I'll never have to endure Bill again. I'll go back to Russia and assume a new name. I'll be free!

A tinge of regret dampened her spirits as she realized she had patients she would be deserting and a cadaver that may have been poisoned with an untraceable poison. Her mind went into overdrive as she hurtled through the night toward West Virginia. She put the Morrows' address in the GPS and gunned the engine, going even faster. A siren screamed in her ears. A blue light flashed. It was the police. She pulled over.

Boris slowed down. He passed her car and parked about half a mile ahead on the side of the road where he could still observe her car.

A tall, burly police officer stopped his police car behind her and jumped out. He ran to her front window and tapped on it.

Svetlana froze in fear. Then she noticed that he was Black and breathed a sigh of relief. He might be nicer than the others, she hoped.

She rolled down her window.

"Driver's license, ma'am."

"Yes, Officer," she said, realizing she had a recognizable Russian accent.

Delving into her Prada purse, she found her wallet and yanked out her license. She handed it to him.

The officer scrutinized both her and the driver's license. "Why were you speeding? I clocked you at ninety-five." He stepped back to seem less threatening.

She looked into his eyes beseechingly. "I have a very sick patient, Officer."

"You're not going in the direction of any Washington, D.C. hospital."

"His name is Walter Morrow. He was released prematurely…I received a call…"

The officer's eyes widened. "You mean Senator Walter Morrow?"

"Yes," she nodded her head in affirmation.

"Okay. I'll just write up a warning this time because you're a doctor, and he's"—his voice caught—"a man of the people." He scribbled out a warning and tore it off his pad, handing it to her. "But observe the speed limit, or *you* could end up in the hospital. You're a doctor. You should know better!"

"Yes, Officer. I don't know what came over me." Svetlana nodded her head with respect. "Thank you for cautioning me. We have no speed limits on our freeways in Russia, but I'll observe the limits here. I'm so concerned about his well-being…"

The police officer cracked a big grin. "No speed limits in Russia? I've got to see that to believe it, but you got to help him, and God bless."

The "God bless" surprised Svetlana. She smiled and nodded her head.

"God bless you too, Officer, and thank you for understanding."

"We're here to keep the peace. Good luck to y'all!"

They exchanged grins. He motioned for her to take off, making sure the traffic was clear. Svetlana gunned the engine and pulled back onto the freeway, careful not to exceed the speed limit. She realized that she was driving dangerously and felt grateful that the officer who pulled her over had been so nice.

As she continued to drive toward West Virginia, the lovely broad-leaved trees that lined the freeway calmed her nerves. She began to breathe evenly. She realized that she loved the United States minus her husband, soon-to-be ex-husband.

Boris pulled out and continued to follow her car.

After driving for what seemed like hours, she reached the town the Morrows lived in and turned off the freeway. The clock on her dashboard read three forty-six when she pulled into their driveway, thinking she'd sleep in the back seat until morning.

She threw a blanket over herself in the back seat, falling instantly into a deep sleep.

Boris parked his car in front of another house and slumped over the steering wheel, exhausted. He fell into a dead man's sleep. His head throbbed from where it was hit when Svetlana ran into the tree.

When Walter Morrow went out to retrieve the morning paper a few hours later, he wondered why a fancy Porsche was sitting in his driveway. He walked over to it, holding onto the newspaper with headlines that announced the death of a patient from an unknown substance. When he saw Svetlana's inert form in the back seat, he put his hand to his mouth.

"Merciful heavens!"

He ran back to the house to get Ellie, who was fixing coffee and scrambling eggs.

"Ellie, there's a woman asleep in a car in our driveway!"

Ellie dropped the spatula she'd been scrambling the eggs with. "What?"

She turned off the flame under the pan and ran to get her coat.

Together, Ellie and Walter Morrow walked out to the car and looked at the sleeping woman.

"What is she doing here?" She turned to her husband with a look of consternation.

Noting the expensive car, she doubted that this was a miner's wife.

"Should we wake her?" asked Morrow, not wanting to disturb the woman.

"Yes! It's too cold to sleep outside in a car. She must be half frozen."

Various thoughts ran through Walter Morrow's head, which felt a lot like scrambled eggs as he tapped on the car window next to the woman's tousled hair. He couldn't make out her face.

Svetlana stirred at the sound of the tapping. She was still groggy from the long drive and short sleep, not to mention the fight she had with her husband. She turned and looked up to see Morrow peering down at her. Taking a deep breath, she sat up and motioned for him to go away. She didn't want to do anything but sleep.

Walter took a step backward, sorry that he disturbed the woman who looked very much like Dr. Jameson.

He turned to his wife. "It's Jameson's wife," he said.

Ellie did a double take. "Why didn't she knock on our door?"

She walked up to the window and tapped on it. Svetlana saw a concerned woman gesticulating for her to get out of the car. She shook her head and then realized she needed to give an explanation.

Svetlana rolled over and opened the door. "I'm terribly sorry. I didn't want to wake you, so I slept in the car. I drove until three in the morning, and I'm exhausted."

She pushed her hair out of her face, hoping she at least looked sane.

Ellie put her hand on Svetlana's shoulder, concerned. "We have a bedroom you can sleep in. You'll catch your death of cold out here in this car. Please come in."

Svetlana nodded dully, unable to assimilate the woman's intent. Slowly she pulled the blanket down, found her shoes, and put them on. She managed to stand up and smile although she felt groggy from lack of sleep and stress. Morrow stepped forward.

"It's me, Walter Morrow, and this is my wife, Ellie!" He beamed at her. "We want you to be comfortable and warm. Please come in!"

He offered his arm for support. Svetlana took it, hobbling through the snow in high heels to the Morrows' comfortable-looking brick house. She took out her cell phone and made a quick call to the hospital to ask for emergency leave.

They guided her up the stairs to a bedroom where Ellie pulled back the thick covers of a double bed. Svetlana took off her wet shoes and sank into it with a look of gratitude. Ellie pulled the covers over her and tiptoed out of the bedroom.

She looked at her husband, who was as confused as she was. "I wonder what could have happened that made her drive here at three in the morning?"

He shook his head in wonderment. The world had stopped making sense to him.

Svetlana dreamt that someone was trying to kill her with a jagged knife and woke up with a start. She looked around the homely small bedroom furnished with crocheted granny blankets on her bed and a hooked rug on the floor. She felt like she was in a time warp. The night's events reeled in her head; she remembered her husband hitting her, the borscht she threw on him, and her crazed drive to West Virginia, to the home of the very person her husband resented the most, the man he unseated to become a senator. She threw off the granny-heirloom crocheted blanket and got out of bed, straightening her tight skirt and blouse as best she could. She teetered out of the bedroom, looking for a bathroom. After trying a couple of door-knobs, she found one. Ellie heard Svetlana's footsteps as she prepared lunch. It was almost noon. She put down the bread and ham to go upstairs.

Svetlana turned to see a graying blond head with unusually kinky hair appear in the stairwell. "May I use your bathroom?"

Ellie laughed a deep guffaw. "That's what it's for. Do you want to take a shower? I can get you a towel."

"A shower would work wonders." Svetlana shook her long hair and smiled in appreciation.

She would love nothing more than a shower to wash the feeling of filth off her…and a way out of her predicament.

Ellie went to the linen closet and found a nice, fluffy towel, which she handed to Svetlana.

"I don't know how to thank you for your hospitality."

"We try to help each other out here in Mohegan. Would you like a ham sandwich and a pickle for lunch?"

"I'd love one. I'll be down in five minutes!"

Svetlana grinned at Ellie's reference to helping each other out. She hadn't encountered such concern for her well-being in a long time.

Too long, she thought as she turned on the water and got in the shower, basking in the luxury of hot water cleansing her body.

Her soul would be another matter. Five minutes later, she descended the creaky wooden stairs to the Morrows' kitchen, where they were eating lunch, heads tilted toward one another as if they might be talking about serious matters. Ellie looked up when she heard the footsteps on the stairs, spotting Svetlana's refreshed face.

She ran to get the brandy decanter. She'd already set a place for her at the table.

"It isn't much, but it'll put hair on your chest." Ellie laughed. "You can have a snifter of brandy for dessert if you want."

Walter Morrow laughed at his wife's sally. He loved every inch of her gregarious body.

Svetlana smiled. "I may take you up on that." She sat on the plain wooden chair at the kitchen table with Ellie and Walter, feeling very much at home. "You have a charming house," she remarked while wolfing the ham sandwich down. She was hungry and then some.

Ellie smiled at the compliment. "It ain't much compared to some of the other senators' palaces, but we're simple folk. Even though Walter was a senator for some thirty years, he never changed, never put on those high-hat Washington ways." She beamed at her husband.

"Just wanted to help the little people that Washington tends to overlook. I did my best to help folks keep their pensions and improve safety standards in the mines…Worked for clean coal too."

"Then my husband came in and took them away."

Walter Morrow looked at Svetlana in surprise. "Well…he hasn't helped. Maybe you can influence him to do better by the poor people."

Svetlana pushed her chair away from the wooden table with its checkered tablecloth. She cleared her throat.

Looking intently at Walter, she announced, "My husband and I had a difference of opinion last night."

She arched an eyebrow, hoping he would understand.

"That can happen in the best of marriages…" Walter cleared his throat, feeling out of his depth.

He and Ellie had never once had a difference of opinion, not one that sent her driving into the night.

"He hit me."

Ellie gasped. "How could he?"

Walter stood up and looked out the window at the hilly, pine-tree-carpeted scenery that surrounded the house.

"A man who hits a woman—"

"Is a coward!" Svetlana finished his sentence for him.

Walter turned to face her, his face clouded with anger. "And you're a doctor, a person who saves lives and tends wounds…How could he?"

Svetlana started to pace around the kitchen. Her heels clicked on the wooden floor.

"He's not a nice man. I could say more, but I think you already understand."

Ellie and Walter stared at her, dumbfounded.

"Was he drinking alcohol?" asked Ellie.

She knew some husbands beat their wives if they drank too much.

"He'd probably had a drink or two, but it was more than that. It was about Fort Bener…"

Ellie wiped her hands on her gingham apron. "I've got to check the pie. We're having peach pie for dessert." She smiled with a tinge of apprehension.

"Thank you for going to all this trouble for me," said Svetlana as Ellie disappeared into the pantry.

Walter Morrow furrowed his brow. "I don't think that man deserves such a lovely wife, and he certainly can't be thinking of the well-being of our people. I'm sorry I lost my Senate seat to such a…a…"

"Beast," said Svetlana with a smile.

"What did you say about Fort Bener?"

"He's on the committee that deals with arcane diseases, such as smallpox…"

Ellie came out of the pantry with the pie. She and Walter Morrow exchanged shocked looks.

"Diseases that are locked into tiny vials for safekeeping at Fort Bener."

"So those diseases still exist?" Ellie's eyes widened in dismay.

"Only if these vials get into the wrong hands." Svetlana gave Ellie and Walter a reassuring smile. "That's not likely to happen."

"But it could... Don't you think they should destroy these bacteria instead of keeping them in vials?"

Svetlana grinned at their naivete. "Of course, I do."

Walter stared into her eyes. "We'd like to help you."

He motioned for her to take a seat at the kitchen table. She nodded her head appreciatively and crossed her legs, arranging her dress so that it looked less rumpled. She put her hand on his forearm.

"Walter...um...Mr. Morrow..."

Walter Morrow grinned. "Call me Walter. After all, we're friends."

"Walter, I must return to Russia."

He looked at her in surprise.

"But before I go, I'd like to tell you that my husband has been seeing one of the scientists at Fort Bener...to develop some sort of virus, I think."

Morrow's jaw dropped. "What's his name?"

Before Svetlana could answer, a black Honda pulled into the driveway. Svetlana ran to the living room, looked out of the window, and gasped, terrified. Walter got up to look outside, but she held onto his arm.

"Don't open the door. It could be my husband...or worse!"

Walter Morrow turned his wizened countenance toward her, perplexed. "It's probably a coal miner's wife asking for help."

He walked over to the window to see Boris get out of the car, buttoning his heavy jacket. He exhaled a deep breath and watched it evaporate in the freezing air.

Svetlana looked out of the window. She saw Boris and froze.

"It's Boris!" She ducked her head, running back to the kitchen to hide.

Walter Morrow looked out of the window. He looked at Ellie, who had followed him into the living room. He was perplexed.

"Why, it's Boris, but he's not supposed to be here until six o'clock for dinner tomorrow. We asked him to postpone..."

Svetlana ran up the stairs, yelling, "He's a spy! Worse, he tried to kill me a few nights ago. That's why he ended up in the hospital..."

Boris strode up to the house and knocked on the front door.

Walter and Ellie exchanged horrified looks. Ellie went back to the kitchen to check on the pie and busied about.

Svetlana came down the stairs, flattening herself against the wall in an effort to hide. "This man will stop at nothing. He's been ordered to kill me!"

Walter Morrow shook his head in confusion. "Why would anyone want to kill you, a doctor, a person who saves lives—"

"Because I defected! I was a spy until my daughter was born."

"You have a daughter?" Morrow turned his head from the heavy knocking on the door to shout at Svetlana flattened against the wall.

He felt dizzy. Nothing made sense.

"Don't let him in," hissed Svetlana as Boris continued pounding on the door.

"Let me in!" shouted Boris, standing on the doorstep surrounded by foot-deep snow.

Morrow sat down in his easy chair as if someone had shoved him. He was flabbergasted.

This can't be happening, he thought.

Then he furrowed his brow and clenched his teeth in anger.

Boris pulled his heavy scarf around his neck to keep from freezing, took out his gun, and walked over to one of the living room windows, tapping on it with his gun.

Svetlana stepped away from the wall and ran over to Ellie, who looked at her in surprise as she ran into the pantry.

"Wait for me," said Svetlana, terrified, tripping over her stilettos as she ran after Ellie.

Morrow stood up and went to the window. "Boris, you can come in. You don't have to break our windows. We'll freeze!"

Boris pointed the gun at Morrow. "Open the window."

Morrow looked around for something to defend himself with but found nothing. Tensing up, he opened the window, determined to talk some sense into this man. Boris clambered in, holding onto his gun and falling on the floor. Morrow stared into his eyes, hoping to reason with him.

"You're a man of the people, a sensitive individual. You don't need a gun…What do you want?"

Boris pushed Morrow away with a brusque movement that hurled him to the floor. "Where's Svetlana?"

"What do you want with Dr. Jameson?"

Boris's lip curled into a snarl. "It's time for her to return to Mother Russia." He laughed at his bad joke.

He headed toward the kitchen as Morrow attempted to stand up.

"Stay where you are, or I'll shoot!"

Morrow shook his head in disbelief. "Boris, you've gone crazy. You'll regret this. Why don't you have something to eat and talk this over? I was a senator. I can help you."

Boris kicked him in the shins and scoffed. "I'm on an assignment, you moron!"

He stalked toward the kitchen, kicking over a footstool as he went, his gun lowered. Svetlana and Ellie ran into the pantry. He heard their heavy breathing. A can fell off the pantry shelf. He stopped in his tracks.

"Svetlana? Come out, or I'll shoot!"

Morrow stood up with difficulty. "Put that gun down!"

Boris turned and pointed the gun at Morrow. He grabbed a wooden chair to defend himself.

A gun barrel emerged from the pantry and fired. Boris went down, wounded, writhing on the floor, clutching his chest. Svetlana rushed out of the kitchen to tend his wounds. She ripped some material off a dish towel and made a tourniquet with dexterity.

"Bitch!" moaned Boris.

With a huge spasm, he convulsed on the floor. Svetlana tightened the tourniquet. Boris lay on the floor, breathing fitfully.

Svetlana leaned close to his ear as she continued tightening the tourniquet. "Who killed my husband?"

Boris breathed with difficulty. He looked at her in supplication.

"I had nothing to do with it," he pleaded.

She loosened the tourniquet. "Who did? Tell me, or I'll leave you to your fate."

Boris looked at her, terrified that he might die. "Our great leader."

"When he was still in the KGB?"

"The orders came from the top. It had to be him."

Svetlana tightened the tourniquet, as well as the expression on her face. "That...that traitor!"

"I'm sorry." Boris breathed with difficulty.

Svetlana laughed an insane laugh. "I'll get him!'

Boris looked at her and began to convulse. She turned him over and massaged his muscular back to calm him. He quieted down, breathing with less effort.

Ellie ran out of the kitchen, still holding the shotgun. "I didn't mean to hurt him!"

She was visibly distraught, her face as red as a beet. Walter Morrow ran to her and held her in his arms.

"It's all right. You saved our lives! Boris was acting like a lunatic!" He kissed her on the forehead.

Ellie looked at him with tears running down her cheeks. "I'm not a murderer!" She began to cry.

Morrow grabbed Boris's gun and put it on the coffee table.

Svetlana took her hand, placing her fingers on her wrist to take her pulse. "You're not a murderer. You stopped a vicious spy from killing your husband! You're a hero! Let me make sure you're all right."

Ellie slumped down onto the sofa, dropping the shotgun.

Svetlana took her pulse and assessed her vital signs. "Do you have high blood pressure?"

Ellie sniffled. "I don't know."

"That man had a gun. He threatened to hurt Svetlana and me. You saved her life, sweetie. Mine too. We're going to call the police, and everything will be all right."

Ellie looked into his eyes, the eyes of her husband she'd trusted for over fifty years. She hugged him close.

Svetlana got up and looked at Boris, wondering what to do with this Russian spy. Her mind raced as she thought of what he'd revealed about her husband's death.

Walter helped Ellie sit back down. "Don't worry. You did what you had to do."

Ellie put her face in her hands as she slumped on the sofa.

Walter Morrow was already on the phone, talking to the local police, who he knew well as Mohegan was so small that almost everyone knew each other.

"Could I speak to Sergeant Smith?" He turned to look at Ellie and Svetlana, who were crumpled on the sofa, suffering from shock. "Yes, hello, Joe, this is Walter Morrow. I'm fine, thanks, but you've got to come out here."

There was a momentary pause. Walter glanced at Boris's inert form and sat down, going into shock himself.

"Joe, we had… You won't believe this… Ellie shot a man! A spy! A Russian spy! Yes, come over immediately!"

He hung up the phone and put his head in his hands. Distraught, he joined Ellie on the sofa, pulling her into his arms. She sighed and began to breathe easier.

Within minutes, there was a knock at the door. Morrow got off the sofa with difficulty and walked over to let the police in. Two Mohegan policemen walked in and surveyed the scene. They spotted Boris's body on the floor and Ellie's shotgun nearby.

Ellie started to cry again. "I only shot him to save my husband and…Svetlana."

They walked over to the sofa where she sat, still in shock.

The policemen exchanged looks. They started to speak at the same time. "*You*, Mrs. Morrow? How could you have shot this man? I mean—"

"You mean that women are supposed to bake pies instead of protecting their spouses with lethal weapons," remarked Svetlana, giving them a sidelong glance.

The heavyset older one looked at her. "It's hard to believe, Miss…Could you give us your name?"

"Doctor Svetlana Jameson." She took a deep breath and prepared to answer their questions, which she knew would revolve around her nationality, her husband, and her whereabouts.

Walter Morrow stepped between the police and Svetlana. "She's a very decent person."

"What's she doing in your house?" The officer took off his hat and scratched his head in disbelief.

Ellie stopped sobbing long enough to utter, "She's our guest."
She stood up and walked over to stand by Svetlana, proud and erect.

"All right, all right, but who is this man lying on your floor?"

Boris groaned, rolled over on his side, and managed to sit up.
"I'm Boris."

The police walked over to him and checked his identification.
"You don't sound like you're from Mohegan."

Svetlana laughed.

Boris raised his head and said, "I'm from Moscow."

The officers grinned. "Nope, you're not from Mohegan."

One of them checked a list of suspects from Russia on his cell
phone. He looked up in surprise. "Jesus. You're wanted."

Ellie hardly heard the police officers because she was so upset.
"I shot him with me trusty shotgun to save Wally's life!" She walked
over to her husband, putting her arm around his waist.

Morrow reciprocated, putting his arm around Ellie's shoulders.
"My Ellie saved our lives. This man barged into our house and…
after insulting Svetlana—Dr. Jameson, that is—took out a revolver
and was going to kill her. He pointed it at me…"

He and Ellie exchanged somber looks.

The officers examined Boris; they saw the gun on the coffee
table.

"What was a Russian…spy…doing in your house, Senator?
Nothing like this has ever happened in Mohegan before."

Svetlana stepped forward, facing the officer. "I can explain.
Allow me to introduce myself. I'm Dr. Svetlana Jameson, the wife of
Senator Jameson."

The officers exchanged surprised looks.

"And this man wanted to…to wipe me out."

"She's lying!" shouted Boris, flapping his unwounded arm like a
chicken. "Don't believe a word she says. She's the spy!"

He tried to sit up, but a spasm seized him. He convulsed and
fell flat on his back, dead as a doornail. Everyone crowded around.
Svetlana gave him CPR, but it was useless. He was lifeless.

Walter and Ellie looked at each other in horror. Svetlana took a deep breath. The police started to draw a chalk line around Boris's body.

"This will have to go to court. Everyone must tell the truth! You will tell the truth, and so will we! We expect everyone to get treated like any other citizen of the United States!" Walter Morrow raised his head with pride.

Ellie stared at him in rapt admiration.

"Then you'll have to come to the police station for questioning, Senator—I mean, Mr. Morrow."

Morrow looked at Ellie, who nodded at him.

"Let's go," she said, letting go of him to look for her winter coat.

Morrow picked up his coat and hat; they walked out the door with Svetlana and one of the policemen while the other called for help on his cell phone, what with so many people on their hands.

Ellie lowered her head in despair. "I didn't want to hurt anyone, but he was going to shoot my husband." She sniffled and tried to wipe her nose on her coat sleeve.

Svetlana followed as they crunched through the snow to the police car.

"Boris was a Russian spy on assignment," she insisted once they were seated in the police car.

She continued to describe Boris as a member of the KGB on assignment to kill her because she had defected and escaped to America.

The policemen exchanged wary looks. This sounded like something they made up in Hollywood; but things like that didn't happen in Mohegan, West Virginia, a small rural town. Arriving at the police headquarters, the woebegone Ellie and Walter Morrow tried to explain what happened in a jumble of words. The desk sergeant's jaw dropped. He was nonplussed. He scratched his balding head and made a call.

"Thanks, Joe. You're right. If the victim was really a Russian spy, this is a matter for the FBI. They'll determine his innocence or guilt. I'm going to hand your case over to the FBI, Walter," he said. "They'll know what to do if he was a spy."

Svetlana stepped forward and, with a thick Russian accent, said, "I can prove that he was. We worked together for the KGB in Moscow. He had orders to kill me."

Walter pulled Ellie into his arms. The police officers looked dazed. They couldn't believe their ears.

"Will you testify in court?" asked the desk sergeant.

"Of course!"

Ellie started to sob.

Morrow held her close, rubbing her back to comfort her. "You saved our lives. You shot him in self-defense."

Ellie continued to sob.

The officers exchanged bewildered looks.

Chapter 8

Senator Bill Jameson lay asleep in his comfortable bed. He snored a bit, then began to dream that he was singing "Mary Had a Little Lamb" in front of the Senate again.

Morrow laughed at him, holding his sides and pointing his finger. "Here's your new senator." He could barely contain his merriment.

The other senators nodded their heads and laughed. Jameson couldn't stop singing despite himself. Soon the entire Senate was roaring with laughter. He was a laughingstock. He was unfit for office. He was—

Jameson tossed and turned in a frenzy. Then he woke up, his eyes wide open. He rubbed them hard to try to regain control of his senses.

It was just a dream…just a dream.

Try as he might, he couldn't calm the anxiety provoked by the dream.

It's Morrow! I've got to…to silence that little twerp for ridiculing me.

He got out of bed and walked to the bathroom, where he stared at the medicine cabinet. He opened it to look for some aspirin as he now had a horrible headache. He brushed the bag containing the vial of…of a lethal poison. He took it out and looked at it.

Where's Svetlana? he wondered.

He stalked into the living room to see if she was sleeping on the sofa; surely she'd come back home. No Svetlana. He slumped onto the sofa, falling back to sleep, his body spread-eagled, too big for the sofa so that he looked like a wild animal, a creature not quite human.

When the rays of the morning sun awakened him again, he shivered, looked around, and wondered what he was doing on the sofa. He glimpsed the paper bag with the vial in it. Shaking his head, he stood up unsteadily, wrapping his bathrobe around himself and heading toward the kitchen to make some coffee.

I need to think clearly…need to get rid of that mealymouthed, mothballed Morrow ran through his mind.

He remembered that he accepted a dinner invitation at his home for that evening.

Perfect, that might work, he thought groggily, looking at the paper bag, which he inadvertently had clutched in his hand.

A smile brightened his face as dark thoughts spun through his turgid mind.

In the kitchen, the sun cast its golden rays on the kitchen nook table where he and Svetlana normally had breakfast. He put his coffee on the nook table and slid a plate of hastily scrambled eggs next to it.

Where's the damn ketchup? That bitch did come in handy at times, he mused as he sat on the bench in the nook.

He gobbled the eggs in record time, remembering he had to appear in the Senate today by one o'clock for some damn vote. He knew he'd vote with his party; it was a helluva lot easier than reading those tiresome bills. Running his hand through his tousled hair, he smiled.

Too bad I have to dine with Walter Morrow tonight, the drudge of working-class crud.

He dressed with care, making sure he'd fit in with his colleagues in the Senate—a suit but not too formal: red, white and blue tie for patriotism, but no silk, and a flag pin. He fastened his diamond-stud cuff links with a grin.

I can always get away with these. Wonder how they're doing in the diamond mines in South Africa?

He giggled at the thought of the child warriors that had been created in Sierra Leone, another diamond-rich but impoverished country.

Pulling onto the Beltway, he heaved a sigh of relief. He loved the tree-lined drive into Washington, D.C. Within half an hour, he handed his car keys to a valet, who nodded his head in deference.

"I have to go to dinner in West Virginia, so make sure my car is waiting at five. And make it snappy." He lifted his head a bit higher to show he knew he was dealing with an underling, a mere valet.

As he strutted away to take the Senate elevator, the valet eyed a buddy. "They get all the breaks, and we barely make the rent."

The other valet rolled his eyes. "Don't I know it! Never gotten a raise in the ten years I been here! What a racket!"

They bumped fists.

Jameson took his seat in the Senate and answered aye to the roll call. He exchanged nods with those around him. The senator at the podium had a monotonous voice; Jameson fell asleep. When it was his turn to vote, his colleague had to elbow him awake. Jameson looked up, startled.

"Vote no," murmured the senator sitting next to him, an older fellow who sometimes wondered how these boy wonders got elected.

He's got big corporations backing him, he mused, annoyed that he had to work so hard for his seat without much assistance.

He was from Wyoming, where there weren't many large firms.

Jameson grunted no and yawned, stretching his arms. He shot the senator who'd elbowed him an annoyed look, stood, and made his way out of the Senate in search of coffee. He'd done his duty by voting no on an environmental bill to put the snowy plover on the endangered list.

What in the hell is a snowy plover? Some kind of bird? Who needs them?

He spotted a page and told her to get him a latte. His mind slowly remembered that he was having dinner with the Morrows this evening. The page, a slight brunette wearing blue-rimmed glasses, smiled at him as she proffered his latte, even stirring it for him.

"Don't stir my latte!" Jameson made a note of the twenty-something page so that he could say something to the other senators to get her fired.

The other pages were prettier, except for the boys of course. He wasn't interested in boys.

He sat on a chair and sipped the latte, wondering how he could cross Morrow off his list, a list of people who had annoyed him.

Morrow was at the top of this dubious list. Jameson couldn't stand to be slighted. Morrow had gone too far. And Svetlana? His mind boggled at the thought of his beautiful foreign wife hurling boiling borscht at him. He fingered the vial in his coat pocket, put his latte down, and strode to the valet station to get his car. If he started early, he could avoid the interminable rush hour at five o'clock.

Hailing the valet at his station, he gave him the ticket stub for his car, repeating, "And make it snappy!"

The valet rushed to find the BMW Jameson drove, worry written on his face.

We've been fired by people like him, he thought as he slid into the driver's seat and gunned the engine.

He pulled the car smoothly into the valet station where Jameson waited, hands on his hips to show his impatience.

"Here's your car, Senator. Is there anything else I can do for you?"

Jameson scowled at him. "Make it snappier next time."

The valet jumped back, saying, "Yes, Senator! Have a nice evening!" He smiled as best he could, hoping for a tip.

The valet waited a few seconds. Jameson got into his car and roared away.

The valet flipped him the middle finger. "Cheapskate!"

Jameson zoomed off, making it to the Beltway in record time. He put Morrow's address in his GPS.

Mohegan? Where the hell is that? Morrow is so tedious.

An errant thought ran through his mind as he passed Georgetown. He turned off the freeway to visit Maggie. Within an hour and a half, he pulled into Morrow's driveway, Khadija by his side in a bright-pink Gucci dress that left little to the imagination, noting with disdain how ordinary Morrow's brick house was.

What a hick. He snickered.

Inside the house, Ellie prepared dinner with Svetlana helping her. Ellie's hand trembled a bit as she added salt and pepper to the roast beef.

"Let me take over," said Svetlana. "You've suffered a severe shock today and should be resting in the living room with your husband." She put a gentle hand over Ellie's and poured juice over the roast.

Ellie looked at her. "Oh, I'm not myself today. You're right. I shouldn't be cooking. Too many knives, and I'm still shaking... Thank you, Mrs. Jameson. I'm right grateful that you're here." Ellie smiled weakly.

"I'm the one who's grateful." Svetlana grinned, taking command of the roast. "Just rest with your husband and regain your composure. You did me an inestimable favor today. Boris was a KGB spy whose orders were—Well, enough of Boris. Just make yourself comfortable in your own home." Svetlana nodded her head in respect.

"Don't mind if I do. You're right. I'm in no condition to handle cutlery and heavy dishes..." Ellie drifted into the living room and sat on the sagging sofa, staring at a picture of the Allegheny Mountains on the wall.

Walter Morrow put down the newspaper and smiled.

"Svetlana has offered to fix dinner for us."

"She's a kind woman. Let's just enjoy a good meal and then get a good night's sleep. You look all tuckered out."

They talked over the day's events. Walter tried to calm his exhausted wife. Just before dinner was ready, they heard a car park in their driveway.

Morrow took a deep breath of frustration. *Not another...*

There was a loud knock on their front door. Walter got up to answer it with a slight groan. His arthritis had been more painful than usual today. He opened the door to find Bill Jameson standing straight and tall in front of him with a very beautiful, very young Black girl who looked half his age.

"Why, Senator Jameson! I thought you were coming later—"

"You said Tuesday, the sixth," replied Jameson, irritated.

"No matter. I'd forgotten. Come in. Do come in." Morrow opened the door wide for him and Khadija.

Svetlana froze in the midst of ladling thick gravy into a gravy boat.

Jameson looked around the quaint house with a bit of a grin. He could feel the vial of nerve poison rub against his chest through his jacket.

"I thought we could talk about workers' rights over a drink before dinner."

"Why, certainly," said Morrow, raising an eyebrow in surprise. This seemed premature, but he was pleased that Jameson brought up the subject. "What's your preference? And who is this young lady?"

"Vodka, if you've got any. Her name is Khadija. She's a page." Jameson took off his jacket and made himself at home on the overstuffed sofa.

Khadija stood alone, not knowing where to sit.

Jameson slapped the sofa cushion next to him, beckoning for her to join him. "She can have some vodka too."

Svetlana stood frozen in the kitchen.

"What's the matter?" asked Ellie.

Svetlana put her fingers to her lips to hush her. She pushed the gravy boat aside and ran into the bedroom. Ellie ran after her.

"What's wrong?"

"He's going to harm us!" whispered Svetlana, taking Ellie's arm. "I know him. He hates your husband and only came here to do something *nefaste*."

"What's *nefaste*?"

"Cruel, mean, insidious…"

Ellie opened her mouth in surprise. "Like the other man?"

"Yes!" hissed Svetlana between her teeth as she looked for a weapon—or maybe a window to escape from.

She looked around the room furtively for Ellie's shotgun, which has already been apprehended by the police.

"I've got to escape. Can you divert their attention while I run to the back of the house?"

Ellie stared at her, stunned. She didn't know what to think or do, but she wanted to help Svetlana.

Meanwhile, the two men lit cigars and made small talk in the living room. Ellie ran into the kitchen to stir the peas. It was still an hour before dinner, but she always prepared well in advance just in case someone got hungry early. She listened at the door as the men talked.

"You must meet my wonderful wife, Ellie."

Ellie appeared with an ashen look on her face.

"She's had a bit of a rough day." Morrow chuckled as he stood to introduce her.

"I need your help in the kitchen!" Ellie shouted at the top of her lungs.

Her husband looked at her in surprise.

"As I say, she's had a bit of a rough day…"

"How rough?" asked Jameson, arching an eyebrow and hoping for something interesting.

Ellie pulled her husband toward the kitchen. "Come quick! The roast is burning!"

Morrow gave her a startled look, realizing she was trying to communicate something to him that she didn't want Jameson to hear. He followed her, excusing himself to Jameson, who shrugged and took another puff on his thick cigar.

Ellie took him into the kitchen where Svetlana waited.

"Something's wrong! What is it, Svetlana?"

"Show him another room while I escape. He's my husband. He wants to harm me. He's a dangerous man."

Ellie and Walter nodded, wondering what in the world she was talking about. So much had happened today, but this flummoxed them. Walter went back into the living room, shaking his head. He stared at his guests, perplexed.

"Um, let me show you my photos from the Senate," he said, hoping that might interest them.

Jameson looked up at him, also confused. "Why would I want to see your photos?" Jameson gave him a withering look.

"They're wonderful photos of Washington, D.C. before they gentrified it," said Morrow, trying to pull Jameson off the sofa by his arm.

Jameson pulled his arm away. "Okay, okay, if you insist. Come on, Khadija."

They got up and followed Morrow into the den, where he kept his favorite photos of himself speaking in the Senate.

Ellie peered out of the kitchen to see if the coast was clear. No sign of anyone. She gave a thumbs-up to Svetlana.

"They're out of the living room."

Svetlana gave her a furtive look, yanked the shawl off Ellie's shoulders, and made a mad dash for her car. Ellie ran after her only to hear a car roar away. She looked at the front door, her mind a blank, shivering because she needed a shawl over her shoulders.

As Svetlana drove away from the Morrows' house, her mind cleared. She realized that her husband very likely meant to harm them. She thought of the vial he'd hidden in the medicine cabinet. Slowly but surely, her doctor's instincts prevailed. Slowing the car, she turned it around and headed back to the Morrows' house. Her fear of her husband melted like snow on a warm day as she determined to thwart any *nefaste,* evil plans he likely had planned. Parking her car outside their home, she saw some old, rather worse-for-wear pickup trucks parked in his yard. Confused, she remained in her vehicle, pulling Ellie's shawl around her shoulders as she tried to fathom what was going on.

Some rather shabbily dressed, rough-hewn men got out of the pickup trucks. Svetlana realized they were likely miners and friends of the Morrows. She felt relieved. They could be allies.

Jameson and Khadija walked into the living room with bored looks on their faces. Walter Morrow beamed, chatting about times past—about his accomplishments, workers' rights, civil rights, and clean coal mining laws he authored and helped pass. When he saw Ellie standing stock-still as if she'd seen a ghost, he stopped dead in his tracks.

"What's going on?" He put his arm around Ellie's shoulders. "Where's that pretty shawl I gave you for your birthday?"

Ellie just shook her head at him. She remained mute, stunned by the turn of events. She pulled him into the kitchen while Jameson sat on the sofa, pulling Khadija onto his lap. She struggled to no avail. He had a firm grip on her waist.

"You...child molester!" she hissed.

Jameson laughed as she tried to free herself.

In the kitchen, Ellie whispered, "Svetlana says Jameson wants to harm us. She just drove away in her car, and that girl he brought can't be more than sixteen years old."

Morrow scratched his head, wondering why Jameson would want to harm them and why Svetlana would take off without thanking them.

"She was scared stiff," said Ellie.

He nodded, trying to understand these very strange people. In all his years in the Senate, he'd never met the likes of them.

Meanwhile, the miners and their families trudged toward the Morrows' house. They knocked on the front door. Jameson and Khadija looked up. She pried his hands off her body, pushing him away to answer the door.

"Come back, little Sheba." Jameson laughed as she opened the door wide.

The miners looked at the scantily Gucci-clad teenager in surprise. No one ever dressed like that in Mohegan.

"I'm a dinner guest," she said with a wink.

They looked her up and down and smiled. They figured Morrow was hosting one of his daughters' fancy college friends. She let them in, much to Jameson's consternation. Ellie wandered out of the kitchen to greet them. She whispered that there might be an unscrupulous guest at their dinner table. The miners and their families nodded. Some of them stayed outside, sneaking around to the dining room window to spy on the guests while other miners arrived.

"We heard someone tried to kill Wally today," one of them whispered in Ellie's ear.

"And you plugged him," chuckled another.

Ellie grinned. Walter came out of the kitchen, looking a little out of his element as he joined his wife.

"Who is the man in the dining room?" asked one of the miners' wives.

"Your new senator, Bill Jameson," whispered Ellie with a smirk.

Their eyes widened, and they exchanged looks. Some went back to their pickups to get shotguns. There were at least twenty people surrounding the Morrows' house at this point. Those who had guns sneaked up to the house, nodding to the miners at the window. Except for their feet crunching in the snow, they were dead silent.

A thick fog enveloped the house, which suddenly seemed eerie and unnatural. No one felt like talking.

Svetlana's curiosity overcame her, and she got out of the car, walking toward the house. She prayed that Jameson wouldn't detect her presence.

"Just wait a minute. We have some business to tend to," said Ellie.

Walter took Ellie by the hand. They walked back into the living room. Ellie smiled at Jameson and Khadija, who stood nearby.

"I hope you're hungry because the roast beef is ready with lots of mashed potatoes and gravy."

Jameson smiled broadly, fingering the vial in his pocket. "I love a good home-cooked roast," he proclaimed, "and so does Khadija."

She gave him a dirty look. "He has no idea what I like," she asserted.

Walter sat opposite him while Ellie scurried to the kitchen.

"We're having the tomato soup first," she said.

Jameson smiled. "Love tomato soup."

"Would you like some fresh basil in it?"

"Yes, of course," replied Jameson, smiling broadly at Walter.

Walter smiled back as best he could. *What can this man possibly want with us?* He took his checkered napkin and put it in his lap. He took a deep breath, hoping to control his nerves. *Getting a chunk of meat in my windpipe is nothing compared to this.*

Ellie brought out the soup, piping hot. Steam rose from it. Jameson grinned a Cheshire cat grin. She started to ladle soup into the bowls in front of them.

"Oh, I forgot the basil!" She ran back into the kitchen to get it.

Morrow excused himself, pushing his chair away from the table to follow Ellie. He wanted to talk to her.

Jameson stealthily pulled open the vial of lethal poison and put it in Morrow's soup. "That's the last time he'll shake his fist at me." He smiled a devilish grin.

"What's in that vial?" asked Khadija. "What are you trying to do?" She stood up, grabbing the vial from Jameson.

He recoiled. "Don't touch that!"

Khadija threw it at him.

He jumped up, startled. "There's poison—"

"I hope you die of it! You're a rapacious devil who deserves the worst! Your family owned a plantation that owned some of my people. I hate you!" She kicked him in the shin.

"Ouch! Why, you little vixen! I'll see that you never work at Maggie's again! You Black whore! You'll be dead as a doornail!"

Khadija started to chortle with laughter as she thought of Jameson's dead body.

In the kitchen, Walter pulled Ellie aside, whispering in her ear, "He doesn't seem dangerous, yet I know he voted on legislation to cut health care. Listen carefully to what he says. Maybe he wants to make a deal, except I don't know why he'd want to make one with me."

Ellie looked up at him with concern. "He took your Senate seat. Maybe he's afraid you'll get it back."

Morrow smiled at the thought. They walked into the dining room together just as Khadija kicked Jameson in the shin. They looked at her in disbelief.

"What's going on?" asked Ellie.

"This man is evil, the descendant of slaveholders. His people enslaved some of my people!" She hit him again.

"Slavery was legal in those days!" roared Jameson. "Look at her, all tricked out in a filmy little dress. She's a prostitute!"

"I'm not your whore!" yelled Khadija. "And I saw you put something in his soup!"

"What?" Morrow walked over to Jameson. "What is she talking about?"

"Nothing! She's talking out of her piehole," yelled a distraught Jameson.

Morrow's jaw dropped at the use of such foul language.

Ellie walked over to Khadija. "We can help you. You shouldn't have to put up with a man like that!"

She took Khadija by the arm and steered her away from Jameson. Khadija started to cry. It was too much; she couldn't keep the tears back.

Ellie grabbed a napkin from the table and helped her dry her eyes. "Don't you worry. Stay with us. My husband is a good man. He was the senator whose seat was taken by that"—she pointed her finger at Jameson—"that filthy rat!"

Another car with an old engine pulled up outside, making a racket. The family the Morrows helped a few weeks ago piled out in varying degrees of disarray. Their father still limped.

Jameson jerked his head around when he heard the car, thinking it might be Svetlana.

Morrow chuckled. "That must be the Foleys. I recognize the sound of their car engine."

Ellie ran pell-mell to the door and peered into the darkness. "Come on in and have some dinner with us," she trilled, happy to see people she could trust.

Jameson looked at Morrow's soup that had anthrax in it from his vial. His eyes widened as he considered the possibilities. "No, don't let them in! They're dangerous!"

Morrow frowned at him, shaking his fist just as he had done on the stairs of the Capitol building. "These are friends of ours. They're folk who are down on their luck. You represent them in the Senate, don't you?"

Jameson stood stock-still, his jaw agape. "Of course, I do, but now's not the time to talk politics." He looked at the grimy mother and her children standing in the cold night air. "Come back another time. I'm having a serious conversation with Mr. Morrow."

Morrow stood his ground. He edged in between Ellie and Khadija. "We're about to have a serious conversation. You're just the people your new senator needs to hear from. Come right in and have a seat at the table. Ellie, bring some more soup bowls." He scowled at Jameson. *What a nerve this man has!*

Jameson threw his hands in the air as Ellie dashed to the kitchen for more place settings. "There isn't enough food."

Ellie poked her head out of the kitchen door, "Yes, there is! I always cook for ten just in case! We're used to distressed families stopping by to see us!"

"Right in time for dinner, eh?" Jameson said, mad as a wet hen.

He watched out of the corner of his eye as Ellie rearranged the soup bowls and ladled soup from theirs into the mining family's bowls.

The haggard mother smiled at her. "I don't wanna cause no trouble, but Charley's disability check didn't come..."

Morrow took one of the children by the hand and guided her to the table. "You're like part of the family. We're always happy to see you!"

Khadija walked over to the bedraggled mother and proffered her hand. "I'm Khadija."

The Foleys looked at the beautiful young Black girl in an expensive party dress and nodded their heads.

"Where'd you get that dress?" asked the mother in a high-pitched voice.

Khadija laughed. "It's part of my job. I'm on my own and could use some nice folks like you...for family."

"Don't you have a family?"

Khadija shook her head. "My little sister and brother are living on the streets."

"Oh, you poor thing! We'll help if we can! We don't have much money..."

"I'm making a lot of money!" beamed Khadija, raising her head. "I'll tell you about it"—she looked at the dining room table—"after we eat." She whispered in the mother's ear. "Don't touch the soup!"

Jameson looked at the soup bowls and sat down on the sofa.

"Why're you sitting on the sofa? There's room for everyone at the table!"

Ellie was perplexed. His behavior was too unusual.

"I...I've lost my appetite," said Jameson with a glazed look.

Ellie gave him a sly look. "Why, you were hungry enough a few minutes ago! Come on and eat with us. Don't be silly!"

Jameson stood up, offended. "How dare you call me silly, you...you..."

"She saved our lives this morning, this silly woman," interrupted Walter Morrow, annoyed. "She saved your wife's life!"

Jameson sat down at the table, nonplussed. "Svetlana?"

Svetlana, who listened outside the front door, shivered in the cold night air. *I should go in and tell them what's in their soup.* She edged toward the doorway.

"Yes, Svetlana, your lovely wife, whom you've treated badly, very badly," said Ellie with a sneer on her normally placid face. Anger coursed through her heart, making it pound hard in her chest. "Now eat your soup!"

Jameson stared at the slightly unkempt, slightly overweight woman who would never even make it past the butler at a Washington party.

He shook his head. "I don't like tomato soup."

Khadija laughed. "That's because there's something in it, you scurrilous scum, you rotten to the core—"

She started to lunge at him, but Walter Morrow grabbed her by the wrist. She wriggled, angry at being thwarted.

"There's no need for violence, my dear young lady. How do you know there's something other than tomatoes in our soup?"

"Because I saw him empty a vial into it, just yours, but now that Ellie redistributed it, it's in everyone's. I dare you to take the first sip, John!"

The folks outside the window began to get their guns ready in case they had to protect their senator, the coal miners' savior as they sometimes called him.

Svetlana inched toward the doorway as the miners readied their rifles.

Jameson stared dumbfounded first at Khadija, who laughed with a brazen sneer, then at the soup. Slowly he took the soup spoon and dipped it into the tomato soup in front of him.

He smiled a bizarre smile and began to sing, "Daisy, Daisy, all for the love of you..."

Khadija pushed everyone away from him, but he tossed the spoonful of soup at her, hitting her in the face. She jumped up, wiping her eyes. Then she heaved a bowl of soup in his face and streaked into the bathroom in search of an antidote, realizing she was probably a dead duck.

"Call an ambulance!" she yelled from the bathroom.

Ellie and Walter Morrow exchanged terrified looks. Their house had become a house of horrors.

Jameson jumped up from the table, pulling a gun out of his jacket. "Don't move!"

Everyone froze except for the men outside the house, who came bursting in. Jameson fired at them, hitting one in the leg. He fell while the others grappled with Jameson, disarming him in a matter of minutes. Jameson looked at them, his eyes bulging in fury. He was trapped, and he knew it.

"I didn't mean to hurt anyone!"

Svetlana could wait no longer. She hurried through the open door to administer first aid to the bleeding miner.

"Call an ambulance," she said as she ripped some material from Ellie's shawl to make a tourniquet, staunching the flow of blood from the miner's wounded leg.

Ellie ran to the landline phone and called an ambulance and then the police as Jameson struggled to free himself to no avail since two hefty miners had him pinned to the floor.

Amid the melee, Khadija walked slowly out of the bathroom, her dress wet with water, stained with Mercurochrome, her eyes full of tearful anger. "If that vial had what I think it had in it, I'm as good as dead." She walked sinuously over to where the men held Jameson and slapped him in the face.

He roared with laughter. "You're finished!"

She leaned down to look at Jameson. "And you can join me in the grave! What was in that vial? Where did you get it?"

"It was harmless, just medicine for…for my asthma!" yelled Jameson, nearly out of his mind.

"He doesn't have asthma! He's a cowardly, murderous worm!" said Svetlana. "What about the corpse in the autopsy room? I think you know who poisoned him." She crossed her arms in front of her chest, infuriated. "I have an antidote to your poison. Talk and I'll administer it." She looked up in desperation, for she knew of no such remedy.

Mrs. Foley stepped forward. "I know an herbal remedy found in animals."

Khadija looked up at her. "Get it!"

Mrs. Foley ran to Ellie. "Do you have a cat?"

"Why, yes. Samantha is our favorite pet!"

"Get her for me! For the love of God, find her!"

Khadija's eyes bulged in fear.

Ellie yelled, "Everybody, clear out!"

The men from outside looked at her. Two of them held up the wounded man as they walked out of the Morrows' house. An eerie silence fell over them. The moon lit their way as they helped the man into a truck, disbelieving their own ears. Ellie had never acted like that before. They waited, hoping she would call an ambulance.

Mrs. Foley grabbed the cat and squeezed it. The kitty clawed her, then heaved a fur ball onto the rug. She grabbed it and gave it to Khadija.

"Swallow this! It works. I swear it does! It's bezoars."

Khadija took a deep breath and swallowed the disgusting fur ball, an age-old antidote for poisoning. She gagged and coughed, clutching her sides, but it went down. Her eyes bulged.

"It had better work! Gross!" She wiped her mouth on the tiny sleeve of her party dress, drenched with water and spattered with tomato soup. She took a deep breath. "How do you know it'll work?"

"It worked when my grandma got bit by a snake! It's an old slaves' remedy."

Khadija looked at her with admiration. "If it cured slaves, it'll cure me. I descended from slaves. No white blood that I know of."

Ellie came over to them and put her arm around Khadija's shaking shoulders. "You're in good company, sweet pea. My grandma was black as pitch, and my great-great-grandma was a slave. Don't think I'm a cracker."

Svetlana ran to the kitchen to mix a batch of vomit-inducing fluids. She wished she had an antidote for poison with her.

"We know you're part Black! That's why you got kinky hair!" Mrs. Foley laughed.

"Yep." Ellie smiled. "Actually I identify as Black more than white."

Mrs. Foley grinned a big toothy grin at Ellie. "After that night in the graveyard, I knew."

They heard an ambulance siren coming down the country road at sixty miles per hour. It stopped in the Morrows' yard. Two young paramedics jumped out, ready to save a life.

"What's going on?" the shorter darker one asked, looking at Jameson pinned to the ground.

Khadija jumped in front of them. "I've been poisoned by that… that…" She was so angry she couldn't think of how to describe the surly slimeball on the floor.

"Let go of me. I'm a senator! I think I've been poisoned too!" yelled Jameson, writhing in fury.

"We'll get you to the hospital as fast as we can," said the taller paramedic.

He motioned to his partner, who had already wheeled the gurney out of the van. They strapped Jameson to it. Then they saw the miners holding the man who had been shot.

One of them ran to him and took his pulse. "He's still alive! Call another van!"

Ellie stepped between them and the wounded man. "Call the police too! This man shot him!" She pointed to Jameson, faint from the thought that the soup Khadija heaved at him might have poisoned him.

"In self-defense," mumbled Jameson, twisting on the gurney in anger.

"We'll have to put all of them in our van," said the taller paramedic. "It's the only way to save any of them."

"It's that poison the Russians use!" yelled Ellie as she stepped away from the gurney with the wounded man strapped next to Jameson.

They looked at each other and groaned. "He's a lying son of a…" said the wounded man.

Svetlana came out of the kitchen with a bowl of fluids. "It could be nerve poison," she said.

The paramedics stared at Svetlana. "Nerve poison?"

"This induces vomiting," said Svetlana, scooping some out with a glass for Khadija. Then she handed the bowl to the paramedics. "I'm Dr. Svetlana Jameson," she said.

Their jaws dropped.

Morrow stepped between them. "Just get them to the hospital. We'll follow you with Khadija. He threw some kind of poison at her. She needs a doctor right away!"

"She's been poisoned too? Can you take her? We're already breaking regulations," said the shorter EMT.

"She needs immediate attention!" Morrow offered his arm to Khadija, who looked stricken.

"That shameless worm," she mumbled.

"What?"

Khadija blinked back tears and said, "Nothing. Just thinking out loud."

"Step on it. She's already delirious!"

Khadija broke loose from Walter's grip and ran to get into the paramedic's van, her Gucci party dress spattered with tomato soup, but stopped at the front door when she saw the police.

The police jumped out of their squad car, ready to question the Morrows.

"What happened, Senator?"

They looked around and were shocked by the disorderly scene. Miners still lingered, and there was blood from the one who had been wounded. This didn't look like Mohegan to them.

"I'm not sure yet, but someone may have tried to poison us." He looked down at the carpet, breathing heavily.

They steadied him, each holding one of his arms.

"Are you all right?" asked the tall, broad-shouldered paramedic who looked capable of hoisting two men, one on each shoulder.

"I think so, but take this young lady to the hospital! She's been poisoned!" said Ellie, livid with rage.

She hated that scurrilous Jameson so much it made her tremble. She held Khadija by the arm in case she felt dizzy.

"Could you explain what happened tonight, Senator Morrow?"

"Yes, I think so. This man tried to poison our soup, but his, um, the young lady interfered. He threw a bowl of poisoned soup in her face. Jameson's wife, Dr. Jameson"—he motioned toward Svetlana, who was helping Khadija drink her potion—"did all she could to save us."

Ellie looked on, eyes wide as saucers, ready to answer any questions they might have for her.

"Will you testify to this in court, sir?"

"With my hand on the Bible." Morrow straightened up and lifted his head in an august manner.

"That's all we need to know. Thank you, sir. We'll take care of the formalities."

"Now take this young lady to the hospital! He threw poisoned soup at her." Ellie was so upset she nearly screamed at them.

"I want to go with you!" wailed Khadija.

Too late. The police had already lifted her off her feet and were getting her into their car as fast as possible.

"If you've been poisoned, we'll take you straight to the emergency room. Call ahead, Bob!"

Bob waited to listen to what Walter Morrow had to say.

Morrow saw Ellie's wide-eyed look and ran over to hold her. They clung to each other.

"This isn't the West Virginia I know," he murmured.

"The world is changing as we speak, Senator. We hope you'll run for the Senate again and help steady the ship of democracy."

The policeman holding Khadija nodded his head in agreement as she squirmed, trying to get loose.

Morrow smiled a wide smile while still holding on to Ellie. "We'll run for decency and justice for miners and working people everywhere!"

The police looked up at him and guffawed. "That's our senator! You've still got the courage to change the world, and we'll back you all the way!"

Morrow stepped forward, with Ellie holding out his hand. "We can do it together! We *will* do it together, Officer! Thank you for your unswerving service to our community."

They shook hands with enthusiasm.

Then Khadija fainted. The police kneeled over her and performed CPR. Their eyes locked. They knew they had to get her to the ER in a matter of minutes. Ellie put her hands to her face; she started to sob.

"Don't worry. We'll get her there in five minutes. Hurry up, Bob!"

Bob whisked them into the police car, and they sped away into the dark night, their police car siren shrieking full blast.

Svetlana collapsed on the sofa. Visions of her daughter in Moscow went through her head. She doubted that she would ever see her again. Ellie opened the front door. She was so worried that Khadija had been poisoned that she could barely see straight. She sat next to Sveta to commiserate with her. Morrow hoped the ER had an antidote. An eerie silence settled over the Morrow's home like a shroud.

Chapter 9

Khadija lay intubated in a private hospital room in West Virginia, her face pale and her dark hair tucked under a cap. Her EKG showed a weak heartbeat. A nurse took her blood pressure and pulse, applying the cuff to her limp arm. Khadija stirred a bit but didn't open her eyes. The nurse walked over to a computer and typed in her vital signs.

Ellie, Walter, and Adelaide sat in the waiting room.

"How did she get involved with Bill Jameson?" asked Ellie, staring at her distraught newfound friend.

Her heart was racing, and she was breathing hard, still stunned by so many near scrapes with death.

Adelaide shook her head. "I've heard there are places where some of these senators go, but I never believed it."

"You mean brothels?" asked Ellie.

Adelaide nodded her head and wiped her brow. "Some men can be brutes—"

"You mean child molesters," interrupted Ellie. "She's not even sixteen!"

"Anything is possible," said Adelaide, looking furtively at the floor. She was on the verge of tears.

"There have always been spies trying to get our secrets...but nerve poison? That's Russian! Svetlana is Russian. Boris was Russian." Ellie gave her a grim look.

"But her husband had the poison. Where did it come from? Did she give it to him?" Adelaide stood up, running her hands through her hair and pacing back and forth like a caged tiger.

Ellie and Walter stared at one another, feeling queasy and out of their element.

"We've got to report this to the Pentagon! They have to get to the bottom of this evil…evil…horrible…" Walter Morrow gasped for breath at the thought of the CIA's biochemical laboratory harboring lethal poisons. "I'm going to contact them now!"

"Will they believe you?"

"We have to start somewhere!"

Walter Morrow stood and took his cellular phone out of his coat pocket to call the Pentagon. Then he remembered that he no longer had a privileged number. He called the other senator from West Virginia, Jim Brown, who always voted for labor rights and shared Walter's political views on the workers' and civil rights.

"Hello, Jim, this is Walter Morrow."

Senator Jim Brown, a stout fellow in his midforties, looked mildly surprised, wondering what Walter Morrow might want. He was in his office in the Senate Wing of Congress. Pages put papers on his desk and smiled at him in deference. He was well respected for his straight-up manner of dealing with issues and his staff.

"Walter! What a pleasant surprise! I've missed my other half, so to speak!" He guffawed and sat down at his desk, ready to listen.

"I'd like to talk to you in private." Walter Morrow ran his hand across his forehead. "I've run into…unexpected, um, information."

"I hear your wife's a good shot," grunted Jim. He pushed the papers on his desk aside.

"So you've heard?" Walter cleared his throat. "There's a bit more to it than—"

"Isn't there always? Where would you like to meet?"

Walter took a white handkerchief out of his pocket and wiped his brow. "I guess it would raise eyebrows if I met you in the congressional building. When will you be out our way? Or we could meet for dinner in DC."

Jim thought for a minute. "I'm snowed under with bills to read and sign or rebut, so if you could drive into the Beltway and meet me at…maybe the old hangout in Georgetown when we were just starting—"

"Good thinking! I'll drive in this evening at about seven. How does that sound?"

Morrow wiped his forehead again. His nerves were shot, and he could feel his blood pressure rising. The doctor told him he needed to take pills to control it, but he thought he was too busy for pills and such. He knew his nerves were shot, and he should get out of the fray. But who would take his place?

"Seven it is. I'll look forward to seeing you again!" Jim smiled at the thought of seeing his former colleague, so sanguine and well informed on workers' rights.

"Got to see Ellie. She's in a bit of shock."

"I can well imagine…Hold on. I'm snowed under, and Ellie's in a bad way. Why don't we wait until the air clears, so to speak?"

"Well, if you think it's best…" Morrow wiped his brow in an effort to clear his mind.

A page put more papers on Senator Brown's desk. He groaned and put his head in his hands.

"Nope. This is too important." He stood up and grabbed his coat. "I'll be in Mohegan within the hour."

Walter nodded and shut off his cell phone.

Ellie talked to the nurse, hoping to get more information about Khadija.

That poor girl! How could she get involved with someone as horrible as Jameson ran through her befuddled brain.

She wondered if she weren't one of those teens who had been caught in an awful child trafficking scheme.

"Do you think she'll be all right?" asked Ellie while eyeing Khadija's inert form, tubes inserted into her mouth and nose. "Does she have a chance?"

"Come back tomorrow. We'll know more then. This is an unusual case." The young male nurse smiled encouragingly at Ellie. "We're calling a poison specialist to help treat her. She's young and in good health, so that's on her side."

He took Ellie aside. She looked into his eyes, hoping he might say Khadija would be all right.

"She almost regained consciousness once," he said. "I don't want to give you false hopes, but I thought you'd like to know."

Ellie looked into his eyes, tired and dispirited. "Did she say anything?"

The nurse bent down to whisper in Ellie's ear. "I heard her mumble something about her sister. Does she have any family?"

Ellie opened her eyes wide. "I don't know, but we're sure going to try to find out! I can hardly believe this has happened. We're from Mohegan…"

"I understand. The world has gotten very complicated since the wars," said the nurse, referring to the wars in Iraq and Afghanistan.

Ellie thanked him and turned to find her husband, who was conversing with the senior West Virginia senator. She walked up to them, a bit unsteady on her feet. They looked up as she approached.

"Ellie's been through so much today. I'd best take her home," said Morrow.

Senator Brown nodded in agreement. "We can continue our conversation another time," he said, politely standing up out of deference to Ellie.

Morrow took her by the arm, thanked the senator, and steered Ellie toward the parking lot.

The senator watched them go, hoping that he could continue his conversation with Morrow as soon as possible. There was no time to lose. He wanted to convince Walter Morrow to run for president. He couldn't think of a more qualified candidate.

Chapter 10

The next day dawned overcast and dark with storm clouds in the sky. Ellie got up to fix ham and eggs for breakfast, putting on her warm fleece slippers and extra-thick bathrobe.

Morrow stirred in bed. "Don't you be hustling about. Let me fix breakfast today."

Ellie turned and took a deep breath. "I'm worried about the young lady. I'll call the hospital after breakfast…some grits under our belts sure to make us feel better."

The thought of ham, eggs, and grits cheered Morrow. He pushed the bed covers aside and got up.

"Let me help you. I don't want you to do too much today. You need to rest up."

Ellie smiled at the thought of rest. "I'll have time for that after the excitement dies down, after I find out that Khadija is going to be all right."

She straightened up to her full height of five feet, eight inches; squared her shoulders; and looked her husband in the eye.

Morrow shook his head, knowing how determined Ellie could be. He loved her for it, but sometimes he worried for her safety. He wasn't prepared for what she had to say this morning.

"I'm going to expose that shameless worm Jameson. I'll get the goods on him from Khadija and where he got that vial of poison… and I want to make a memorial of the hidden slave burial grounds on the old Jameson plantation after…um…after we beat Jameson and are a senator again. I think you're the one who needs a rest more than me." Ellie took a deep breath and steeled her nerves. "With your permission, I'd like to run against Jameson for your old seat in the Senate."

She inhaled sharply. So did Morrow, fully awake after Ellie's declaration. He saw her in a new light, and although he was surprised, he liked her display of determination and grit. True grit. Coal miners' grit. Black grit.

They ate breakfast in silence, each immersed in their own thoughts. Before Morrow had a chance to get dressed, Ellie was out the door, driving to the hospital with a look of anxiety mixed with determination on her face. Morrow watched her go, thinking to himself that she was right about running for the seat in the Senate because she was ten years younger, stronger, and healthier than him. He felt aches and pains he didn't complain about, but he knew Father Time was creeping up on him.

When Ellie arrived, the nurse asked her to wait outside Khadija's room. All kinds of thoughts ran through Ellie's mind: child trafficking, the hidden slave burial ground, her own Black grandmother, and her ancestors who had been slaves. It troubled her, but she felt as if an invisible hand were pushing her, guiding her. She knew not where. The nurse came out of Khadija's room. He smiled at the serious demeanor of the white lady with the kinky blond hair. He recognized that kinky hair; he knew she had Black blood somewhere in her family tree.

"You can see her now."

Ellie looked up at him, surprised. "How is she?"

"She doesn't show any signs of poisoning, just shock. She's going to recover!"

"Well, I do declare if that isn't the best piece of news I've heard all day!" Ellie stood up and grinned. "I want to have a word with her, if you don't mind?"

"Go on in, but be gentle. She's still coming to."

He grinned a big toothy grin at Ellie. She looked like someone's mother, just the right person for a traumatized patient to talk to.

He showed Ellie into Khadija's room, sterile and bright, with Khadija's dark hair against the pillow, her eyes staring straight ahead. When she saw Ellie, she sat up. She still had a monitor on her arm, which she tried to remove.

The nurse hurried over and put his hand over hers. "Don't touch anything. We've still got you hooked up to our system."

"I've been hooked up to enough systems," she retorted, her dark eyes flashing. She was fully awake.

The nurse motioned toward Ellie. "Mrs. Morrow would like to have a word with you, if you don't mind."

Khadija looked at Ellie, whose eyes were wide, beseeching, and kind. "All right. Come on in."

Ellie sat down next to Khadija. "How are you feeling today, Khadija?"

"I'm doing better than I was yesterday." She frowned at the thought of what had transpired yesterday. "Where is that man?"

"Do you mean Senator Bill Jameson?"

"He told me his name was John," sneered Khadija, used to deception and not sure who to trust, but at least this woman had been extra nice.

"John?"

"Where I work, they don't usually give us their real names."

Ellie felt a surge of apprehension course through her. "Where do you work? You're so young."

"They start us even younger than me," snorted Khadija. "Khadija isn't my real name either."

Ellie shook her head, trying to clear it. "What's your real name?"

"Tina Jameson," said Khadija, looking at the ceiling, wondering why she was telling this lady so much about herself.

The nurse took a deep breath, feeling sorry for his young patient.

"Where I work, nobody's on the up-and-up."

"Where...where..." Ellie stumbled over her words.

"It's called the house of last resort. The one you go to when you got no place but the street to go. And you're lucky if they take you in." She sighed. "Most of us end up on the streets, starving and freezing to death at night."

"Homeless?"

"Yeah. We get abused in our foster homes, so we take to the streets and whoring if we have to. Least we get a roof over our head and food in our belly. The extra money goes to our friends or what's left of our family."

Ellie stood stock-still. The nurse closed his eyes and said a silent prayer. The room filled with electric suspense. They braced themselves for Khadija's, or Tina's, story.

Khadija took a deep breath. "There were five of us, me, my little sister and brother, and Mom and Dad. We were fine till they put Daddy in jail, put him in jail 'cuz he was caught driving a friend's car. The police pulled him over, asked him to show his license and all that, but his friend didn't have car insurance 'cuz he'd lost his job. Couldn't afford insurance." She looked at Ellie, whose eyes were riveted to hers.

"Then what happened?" Ellie squeezed her hand to encourage her. "We're here to help you and your family. Don't worry."

Khadija breathed a sigh of relief. A tear rolled down her cheek. "So my mama kept cleaning houses to put food on the table, but she couldn't make enough to feed us and pay the rent. We got evicted. The authorities claimed she was an unfit mother..." She started to sob.

Ellie sat on her bed and put her arm around her. "No such thing," she murmured.

Khadija nodded and heaved another sigh. "Wish you'd seen the social worker who took us away from her..." She started to cry again. She blurted, "My foster mom didn't care much about me, and her husband started coming into my bedroom..." She couldn't go on. She'd dissolved into a pool of tears. "My mama tried to get us back, but they kept telling her she was unfit...She's not with us anymore. My mama disappeared, and no one knows where she is. Don't even know if she's alive."

Ellie squeezed her tight. "So you had to take to the streets because he was abusing you. Then you started making money any way you could because you were hungry—"

"Starving!" interjected Khadija, wadding her dressing gown into a handkerchief to dry her tears.

The nurse quickly gave her some Kleenex.

Khadija smiled. "Thank you," she said in a sweet voice.

There was a knock at the door. The nurse opened it. An orderly whispered that there was a woman who wanted to see Khadija. It was Mrs. Foley, dressed in her best Sunday-go-meeting dress.

"Let her in," said Ellie. "She's part of the family."

The nurse nodded her assent. Mrs. Foley came in and gave Khadija a bunch of daisies she'd picked outside her house.

Khadija took them, wiping her eyes. "Why, thank you, ma'am!"

"You can stay with us," said Ellie. "We'll have the Foleys over to visit all the time. Would you like that?"

Khadija nodded with a big smile. "I won't have to put out for men anymore," she said with as much dignity as she could muster.

"No, sir!" said Ellie and Mrs. Foley simultaneously.

They looked at each other, and Khadija and all three burst out laughing. The tension oozed out of them like dry rot. They laughed, and then they cried. They laughed and cried at the same time. An invisible bond formed between them.

"We gonna be soul sisters," said Mrs. Foley.

"Everything's going to change for the better," said Ellie. "Wally and I will make sure you get to go to school and get what you need to face the world."

"What about my little sister and brother?"

"We'll find them and your mama. Don't you worry anymore. You've been through more than any child should ever have to suffer through." Ellie squeezed Khadija's hand, determined to help her and others in her situation.

She and Wally would change things for the better, she thought. *I can't stand to even think that a girl would have to resort to.* She couldn't bear the thought.

"I'm going to put a stop to this child trafficking when I'm in the Senate!" she announced.

"What?" said the nurse, surprised.

"Oh, just some idle thoughts." Ellie smiled at him. "Some wishful thinking."

"I understand, ma'am," he said, nodding his head in approval.

I'll show her the slaves' hidden burial grounds on the old plantation. We've got to do right by them, thought Ellie, steeling her resolve.

The nurse nodded toward the door. "Visiting hours are over," he said.

Ellie stood up, relinquishing Khadija's hand. "If you can survive what you've been through, you can survive almost anything. You're brave." She leaned in to show her concern, brow furrowed. "How can I find your sister and brother?"

"They come by Maggie's for food and any money I could give them."

"Maggie's?" Ellie looked at Khadija, wondering who Maggie could be.

"Maggie has a house, um, a place that helps shelter us poor street kids…in Georgetown. It's not the nicest place, but she takes good care of us…" Her voice faltered as she thought of Maggie's low-cut dress and inch-thick makeup, not to mention the row of willing young girls waiting for any man that wandered in, even a woman sometimes.

"She must be a wonderful woman." Ellie's face cleared, and she smiled. "I'd like to meet her to join her in helping young women having a rough go of it."

Khadija took a deep breath. "It's not what you think, Mrs. Morrow. It's…it's a fancy brothel."

Khadija looked deep into Ellie's eyes for a sign of disapproval. Instead, she saw a tear course down her cheek.

"Well, I'll be. So that's where you got that fancy dress."

Khadija avoided Ellie's eyes. 'Yes'm," she said.

Ellie took Khadija's hand and patted it reassuringly. "We're going to change her house into a shelter for women. You'll see. She's probably been through more than she cares to admit, and I'll bet she'd like to change. Your brother and sister can stay with her till I make room for them in my house or Adelaide's. I'll tell her she's got to change her business…or go to jail."

"Can she tell us where your sister and brother are? They can stay with us," said Adelaide. "We can always make room."

She nodded her head vigorously and took Khadija's hand in hers. Her face clouded over as she realized what this poor girl had endured. She knew too many children who had left for the big cities and gotten in trouble.

Khadija beamed at them. "Thank you." Another tear rolled down her cheek. "I can't thank you enough. My sister and brother are having such a hard time. You can't imagine how hard."

Ellie murmured, "You're welcome," and turned to go.

The nurse ushered her and Mrs. Foley out the door. Khadija stared raptly at the daisies. She felt as if Jesus himself had descended from heaven to help her.

Chapter 11

Ellie fussed over her kinky hair, trying to tame it into a facsimile of a pageboy hairdo, but it wouldn't cooperate. She looked in the mirror and combed it back the way it was, long and kinked.

So what? she thought, grinning at herself in the mirror as she fastened the beautiful silver barrette Walter had given her to keep it out of her eyes. *Why try to look like everybody else? I'm a quarter Black. I want it to show.*

She pulled her lavender hand-knit sweater around her shoulders, buttoning all but the top button. Her white blouse poked through. Slipping into the comfortable, sensible two-inch heels that she'd worn for years, she was ready. She had a speech whirling through her mind about workers' and women's rights, clean coal, and slave graveyards.

Walter Morrow walked up to her and smiled. "You look too pretty to be a senator." He laughed. He couldn't resist teasing her a bit.

"Now you stop that kind of talk, Wally! It isn't looks that counts. It's the heart of someone who will fight for everybody's rights." She glared at him.

"All right, all right. Just poking a little fun at you. Isn't every day a man's wife decides to run for office."

"Well, this one's decided if that's not too much for you. I thought we'd agreed on it." She turned around, staring at her husband dressed in a three-piece suit. "You can always run instead of me. I just thought—"

He kissed her on the forehead. "You thought right, and I'm backing you 100 percent! I'm proud of you, Ellie. I could crow like a rooster I'm so proud!"

"Why, you old billy goat!" She laughed, and so did he. "We're going to give Jameson the run of his life. He won't catch us unawares this time. Plus, Khadija's got the goods on him."

"Don't forget the way he cozied up to somebody at Fort Bener to get that poison!" Morrow furrowed his deep brow in anger.

"I won't forget anything! That man nearly killed us all. He has no conscience. He's an immoral, lowlife—"

Walter laughed at her getting so riled up. "Cowardly worm!"

Ellie hugged him tightly. "We've got the goods on him, and we're here for the people, for justice, even if it is delayed."

Walter Morrow let go of Ellie and gestured with his right arm held high. "Into the fray!"

"Into the fray!" she echoed.

They raised their heads high, walked out of their house, and got into their electric car. Morrow started it. They drove toward the Mohegan town hall where half the town was waiting for them, so many people that they had a hard time finding a place to park.

When they entered, everyone stood up and shouted hooray. Half of the population of Mohegan was there. Charles and Adelaide Foley sat in the front row with their two tots. Khadija sat in between them. Svetlana sat next to Adelaide. She'd taken the night off at the hospital to support Ellie's run for senator against her husband, whom she was divorcing.

Ellie and Walter waved to them, grinning from ear to ear. They walked up to the podium together.

Walter spoke first, "It has been my honor to serve the good people of Mohegan and West Virginia as your senator for many years."

Everyone cheered.

"Then I lost my seat to Bill Jameson."

Everyone booed. Ellie grinned, pushing her hair off her shoulder, a bit nervous but thrilled to take up the good fight.

"I'm not as young as I used to be, so my sprightly, beautiful, and dedicated wife, the love of my life, Ellie Morrow, will take my place and give Jameson the run of his life!"

The crowd cheered. Hats flew into the air. Some of the women wiped a tear from their eyes at the thought of a woman running for office. They were so used to cooking and cleaning house that they had never contemplated such a thing. It made them proud that one of them was being cheered and honored.

Ellie took Walter's place at the podium. "I know I'm just a homely little homebody, but lately I've hearkened to the call of duty, and I intend to do right by all of you!"

They clapped as she began to speak. The newcomers standing in the back of the hall crept in slowly until there were about twenty of them. They wore sheets with peaked cones that hid their faces.

"She's nothin' but a nigga!" shouted one of them.

Ellie stopped midsentence. "And proud of it," she continued as they walked toward the podium. "What business do you have here? I'm announcing the beginning of my campaign for senator. Who are you, and what do you want?" She put her hands on her hips. "Take those silly sheets off and face me like a man!"

The sheeted figures stopped for a minute. The crowd turned to stare at the intruders. Some of the bolder ones moved toward the Klan, ready to stand in her defense.

"That's no way to treat a lady," yelled one of them.

"Ladies don't run for office!" yelled a familiar voice.

"We know that's you and your cohorts, Bill Jameson," said Ellie, unflinching. "You don't scare us."

Svetlana stood up, turned to face her husband, and shouted, "You're a coward and a cheat!" Her blond hair shone in the light coming through the rafters of the meeting hall.

Jameson turned red in the face under his Ku Klux Klan sheet. "And you're a Jew, begat when Eve fucked the damn snake!"

The crowd sucked in its collective breath in shock. A hefty Black man jumped Jameson, tearing off his sheet, revealing his puffy red face. The rest of the crowd joined him, pulling sheets off the rest of the Klan members in a melee, revealing the town sheriff among others beneath their sheets. Jack Smith ducked behind a car. No one saw him. He breathed a sigh of relief.

"Stop this foolishness," yelled Walter Morrow, beside himself, shaking an angry fist at them.

"I'm running for a seat in the Senate to help all the people, even grown men who act like little boys," crowed Ellie. "Shame on you. You've stalked the vulnerable and stripped them of their dignity because you yourselves are cowards. You act in a mob and plunder those who cannot defend themselves, usually people of color. Shame on you, Sheriff, for joining them. What kind of justice have you given us during the many years you've been entrusted with keeping the peace? Shades of justice. White man's justice. If I'm elected senator, I will vote for every citizen's rights, the right to a fair trial by jury with a jury that isn't jury rigged. We're sick of your vile tricks that have imprisoned and even taken the lives of the innocent throughout the years!" Ellie shook her fist at them, turning red in the face.

The crowd stepped back and stared at Bill Jameson and the other descendants of former plantations owners, known to all for their violent behavior for countless years. Humiliated to the bone, Jameson was shaking.

Ellie walked up to Jameson, whose hair was mussed and suit disheveled. "Shame on you, Billy boy. Now go home and calm down. I fight fair, and I expect you to do the same." She stared him in the eye as the crowd followed her every move.

Jameson looked at the hall full of people and blanched, realizing he'd been humiliated, something he feared more than anything.

"Daisy, Daisy, all for the love of you," sang Walter Morrow, laughing.

Bill Jameson turned tail and ran out of the town hall, mad as a wet hen, yelling, "You're going to pay for this!"

The others ran behind him.

A corpulent fellow with a low forehead caught up with him, catching him by the arm to get his attention. "We can get our revenge right now if you want, boss."

Jameson whirled and faced him, his face red with anger. "How?"

"When that Black girl comes out of the meetin' hall—"

"What Black girl?"

"Har-dira," said the low-browed fellow with difficulty. He hated foreign names that he couldn't pronounce.

"Do you mean Khadija?" Perspiration dripped down Jameson's face. He wiped it with a handkerchief. "She's a no-good slut. Her life isn't worth a plugged nickel."

"So you get what we wanna do."

"Well, don't mess her up too bad. She was good in bed."

Everyone laughed loud and hearty at the thought of blond Jameson in bed with a Black woman.

"She's a slut."

"Okay. So let's get her and teach her 'em a lesson!" shouted Jameson so loud they could hear him in the hall.

Svetlana stood up and yelled, "We will teach you a lesson! Don't you dare touch her!"

"Shut up, bitch," growled Jameson, eyeing Sveta. "You're going to eat your words!"

They got into their cars and drove outside the parking lot, parking on the side of the street to wait. "Let's just arrest them for disturbin'," ventured the sheriff.

"Toss 'em in jail for a night and let them think about their uppity ways! Women running for office, acting like they's as good as men...What a nerve!"

"Yep, I'll lock 'em up," said the sheriff.

He also wanted to protect them from the angered KKK members. He liked the Morrows and respected Walter's work for coal miners. His father had been one. He rued himself for putting on that KKK sheet.

Ellie and Walter Morrow came out of the town meeting hall feeling exuberant, talking to Adelaide and her husband with big smiles on their faces. Svetlana stood next to them.

"You feeling better, Charlie?" asked Ellie.

"I'm working in the shafts again, thanks to you." He grinned. "Reckon we'd better get on home. We get up early."

"I would like to take some x-rays of your leg at the hospital," interrupted Svetlana.

Charlie smiled at Sveta in gratitude. "No need for x-rays. My leg is doing just fine." He turned to say goodbye to the Morrows.

Sveta nodded in acquiescence. She still wanted to see some x-rays of his leg.

"I remember fixing breakfast for Wally when he worked in the mines at five in the morning," said Ellie. "Our girls were still young and had to get them ready for school and such. Adelaide, why don't you come along with me and"—she looked around and saw Khadija standing back, feeling a bit awkward—"and Khadija. Come, ladies. We need to talk. I want you to help me with my campaign." Ellie grinned at them.

Mrs. Foley and Khadija blanched. "Help you? How?"

"Help me turn out the vote, talk to people, and tell them what I want to do for them. Door-to-door stuff...I can pay you! Pay you as best I can from my savings account!"

Khadija limped to Ellie and hugged her. "Just give me a place to live and food to eat. I don't need any money! But if you see it in your heart, you might give some to my sister and brother on the streets..."

She had never completely recovered from the poison Jameson threw in her face. Her spine had been affected, so she walked with a limp. But her brain hadn't been damaged. She was disabled, but she could still go from house to house to get petitions signed and work the phones.

"They're going to move in with Adelaide! We can't have children starving and freezing on the streets. They need to be in school." She thought for a minute. "They can help us!" She grinned at Khadija, putting her arm around her waist.

Khadija stifled a sob of gratitude. "That's the nicest thing anyone's ever done for me!"

Mrs. Foley beamed at them. "I'll be happy to help any way I can."

Svetlana looked on, smiling warmly. She felt at home with these people. "I'd like to ride with you, if you don't mind. I want to check out Khadija's limp once you get home."

"I'll drive home with my Charlie, and you go on ahead. We can talk in the morning. I want to talk to some of my friends to get them to help," said Adelaide.

"Why, that's right nice of you, Adelaide. It would be nice to have a doctor in the house just in case. Ya never know what might happen!"

They laughed at Ellie's sally.

"Are you sure you don't want to join us?"

"Thank you kindly, Mrs. Morrow, but I'll go home with my husband," said Adelaide.

"I'd like to ride with you to make sure Khadija's all right," repeated Svetlana, looking at Khadija, wondering how she had survived nerve poisoning. *Maybe there was something else in that vial.*

Khadija smiled at her in gratitude. "Thank you, Doctor."

"Just call me Sveta."

Walter Morrow looked at the joyous faces, happy as could be. "All right! Don't take the long way home! You know we go to bed at ten."

He watched them bundle into the Tesla, Sveta and Khadija sharing a seat, and pull away, amazed at his wife's daring do. He was proud of her, proud as punch.

The women drove toward the thick woods surrounding them and a crescent moon in the sky. The stars shone brightly. They were chattering about how they could set up a campaign when blinding headlights flashed behind them.

Svetlana sucked in her breath. "Just like the KGB!"

Ellie floored the accelerator; the Tesla surged forward. She took sharp curves at breakneck speed as Sveta and Khadija held hands in fright.

"Drive to the police station," said Svetlana.

"The police are after us right now," replied Ellie as she twisted the steering wheel to miss a signpost on the side of the road. She was doing ninety.

"What are we going to do?" gasped Khadija.

Ellie jammed on the accelerator. "Pray."

The car hit the gravel on the side of the road and swerved, almost rolling over.

"Dear Lord!" said Ellie as she drove like she were in the Indie 500. She couldn't shake them in their custom Porsche.

Svetlana sucked in her breath. "That's my husband's car."

Jameson and a corpulent fellow pulled up alongside Ellie's car as she sped down a narrow stretch of the road, deep in the West Virginia woods. It was a dark and moonless night. Fear crept up her spine. She started to gasp for air.

"Keep calm," said Svetlana. "Always stay calm." She spoke like the experienced doctor that she was.

Slowly but surely, the Porsche crept up beside them.

"Funny-looking car ya got there," yelled the heavyset man.

"And some funny-looking women in it," chimed in Jameson. "Guess you'd better pull over so we can talk!" he yelled above the noise the fat man's pickup truck was making.

The women froze in fear. Khadija was scared to death. She knew these men could be brutal.

"We don't feel like pulling over," yelled Ellie.

She'd rolled down the window. She rolled it back up as fast as she could. A cold shiver ran down her spine. Jameson was up to no good, and she knew it. That was when the Porsche crunched into the side of her car, pushing it into a ditch on the side of the road. Ellie pushed Walter's number on her cell phone, but someone yanked her door open and grabbed the phone out of her hands. Khadija said a silent prayer.

Banging his door shut, the sheriff strode over, puffing his chest out like a bantam rooster. "Why don't you come down to headquarters where we can decide if you're guilty of disturbing the peace?"

He looked down at his polished boots, a bit ashamed but hoping for a decent outcome. He knew the women had done nothing wrong except for ruffling a few male tail feathers. Then a red pickup truck screeched to a halt behind them. Two hefty men with tattoos and a Nazi cross around one of their necks jumped out with sawed-off shotguns.

"We've got ya covered!" yelled the one with the cross around his neck.

"Quit fussin' with them! They ain't worth it," said Jameson's brutish cohort.

He stared the sheriff in the eye, then pulled out a gun and shot Ellie and Svetlana in the head. Ellie slumped over the steering wheel; Sveta slumped onto Khadija, who tried to resuscitate her as blood gushed from her head wound.

The sheriff turned and looked the other way, shocked yet knowing these men would shoot him too if he ratted on them. He felt sick to his stomach.

"The bitches deserved it," said Jameson. "Now I don't have to get a divorce."

"No, but you got to go to a funeral," said the burly man who had shot them.

The men laughed and walked over to the passenger side of the car, staring at Khadija trying to bring Svetlana back from the dead. A burly, three-hundred-pound lump of lard yanked the door open. Khadija screamed so loud that he took a step backward.

"Don't mess her up too bad," said Jameson.

Khadija looked them in the eye. "Murderers! Child molesters!" she yelled in a voice that curdled Jameson's blood.

He hadn't expected Khadija to give such a spirited retort. He felt himself getting hard. He wanted her one last time. He took off his jacket as his buddies yanked her out of the car, fighting with all her tiny might and screaming at the top of her lungs. They started to hit her in the face. She kicked them in the shins and tried to make a run for it, but her legs didn't function like they used to. She couldn't run.

"Hold your horses!" said Jameson.

They looked at him in surprise. "You told us—"

"Give her to me," he snarled with his lips curled like a wild boar.

They pushed her into his arms, and he ripped her dress off as she smacked him in the face.

"Bitch! You're gonna get it!"

They went down flailing and screaming.

"Hold her down while I..."

The men looked at Jameson. They hadn't expected this. They pinned her to the ground. She writhed and screamed bloody murder. Jameson unzipped his pants, pulled her off the ground, and stood her against a tree where he could have his way with her upright and not get dirty in all that West Virginia mud. Khadija wailed as he penetrated her, raping her with a ghoulish smile. She screamed and bit him. When he was through, he let her slide back down to the ground. Khadija picked up a rock and hit him with it as hard as she could. It landed square in his left eye. He yelped and put his hands to his bloodied face. The men rushed to help him, but she'd hit the optic nerve, blinding him. He thrashed about as the men looked on in horror. Jameson tripped and fell on the ground, hitting his head hard on another larger rock.

They tried to pull him up, but he was a deadweight, a corpse. The second blow had killed him. Khadija managed to stand up and limp toward the woods. The men grabbed her. She was naked except for a pair of thong panties, shaking from her ordeal. They were all over her. One of them pulled his pants down and penetrated her once again. Khadija flailed at him and twisted and turned, but he weighed twice as much as she did.

When he finished, she began to cry.

He started to strangle her, but the others pulled him off because they'd always wanted some Black pussy too. Khadija put up the best of fights, but she was outnumbered by some of the biggest brutes in Mohegan. She let out a final scream and fainted from blood loss from a blow to her head and so many penetrations that her vaginal wall had been punctured.

"Hang 'er high!" yelled the burly one in jubilation.

They grabbed her near-lifeless body, looking for a tree to hang it from.

"We fresh outta rope!"

They stopped dead in their tracks. Khadija was still bleeding. Her eyes rolled back in her head.

"She's still alive."

The three-hundred-pounder guffawed. "Lookie here. This looks like a cross." He pointed at two fallen branches that had crossed one another. "Put her on it. She can die slow."

The other men put Khadija's body on the crossed branches and erected it. She lay limp and lovely on it, her head slumped to one side. She hallucinated Christ coming down from heaven to save her as the men erected her on the crossed branches.

"Forgive them, for they know not…" she murmured.

Her eyes rolled back in her head, and she died. One of them threw her bloodied Gucci dress over her body and slunk away with the others, who started to run like thieves. The rhinestones on the dress sparkled in the dark.

Ghosts from the hidden slave graveyard at Jameson's plantation hovered around her, some in supplicant positions as if praying and others reaching out to her, hoping that she would go to heaven.

Chapter 12

Walter Morrow's shoes lay on the floor in front of his weary body as he sat in his easy chair, waiting for Ellie.

Sure is taking her a gosh darn long time to get here, he thought as he sat up in his chair. *Jameson and his boys looked pretty freakish comin' into the meeting hall the way they did. What if? Nah.* He sat up a bit straighter, frowned, and stood up, bending over to put his shoes back on. *That lowlife weasel wouldn't dare...*

He was out the door in five seconds as he remembered how Jameson had tried to poison them. He ran to his car and gunned it out of the driveway and onto the road.

If anyone's touched my Ellie or any of those women, I'm...I'm...

For once in his life, Walter Morrow was at a loss for words.

When he came to the wooded part of the highway and saw a car in the ditch next to the road, his heart started pounding. As he got closer, he saw that it was a Tesla. When he saw Ellie's body slumped over the steering wheel, he jumped out of his car, ran to hers, yanked open the door, and pulled her limp body to him. He hugged her to him and started to cry when he felt her move. She moaned a low, miserable sound, but she was alive. He called the paramedics.

When they arrived, they found Walter giving CPR as best he could to Ellie, with Svetlana's body still in the car. The two rugged tall paramedics took her from him and got her on a gurney and into their van, hooking her up to an intravenous tube. She stirred.

"She's alive!" one of them shouted just as the other pulled Svetlana's lifeless body from the car.

"This lady isn't," said the other as he got her into their vehicle. "She's been shot in the head."

Walter lowered his head to say a prayer.

What about Khadija? ran through his turbulent mind. *She'd been with them, hadn't she?*

"There's another lady with 'em!" he hollered as he stared at the paramedics setting up a lifeline for Ellie. His head whirled. "Call the police!" His heart began to pound like a bongo drum. He went down.

By the time the Mohegan police car pulled up to the grisly scene, the paramedics had revived Walter and sped away with Ellie. They left Svetlana's inert body for the police to examine for evidence.

Walter sat propped up next to Ellie's Tesla while the police peppered him with questions—who, what, where, and why.

He answered as best he could, pointing toward the woods. "You'd better search in there," he said, numbed by so much violence.

His mind faded in and out. *Was Ellie…*

He couldn't bear to think of her no longer with him.

They helped him to his feet and into his car, where he sat behind the steering wheel—dazed, numbed, and distraught.

I got to find my Ellie ran through his turgid mind.

He started the car and drove toward the local Mohegan hospital, where two doctors looked at Ellie's skull in amazement. The bullet had hit her silver eagle barrette, knocking her unconscious but not entering her skull. It had saved her life.

The police plunged into the woods, running through thickets and groves of trees until one of them tripped over something.

His partner shined his flashlight on it and said, "Damn! It's the new senator!"

They stared at Jameson's inert form in disbelief.

"I think we need an ambulance," said the police officer who'd tripped over his bare leg, trousers down.

"What for? He's a goner. We need backup to look for that girl!"

They phoned in for more officers. Soon the woods crawled with police officers and a few Klan members without sheets, hoping to get to Khadija before the police did. Some officers arrived with bloodhounds; and the search was on through hill and dale, scraggly pines, and thickets of berries that stained their trousers as they searched, half crazed for the most part although some had bloodlust urging them on. It was a motley crew.

The dogs started barking like the lions of hell when they mounted a slight rise in the woods. One of them saw something bright in the undergrowth. An officer grabbed it; it was Khadija's pearl necklace that the madam had given her to wear on special occasions.

"I see a pool of blood!" yelled another officer.

"That's from some critter a wolf killed," yelled a Klansman, trying to lead them away from where her body was lying on the crossed tree branches.

He'd carved a KKK onto her chest in the thrill of the kill that he knew would inculcate him and his buddies, the sheriff among them. Too late as he heard a distant howl. One of the officers had found her body with her Gucci dress flung over it. The rhinestones sparkled in the moonlight.

Jack Smith, long and lean, arrived at the scene, slowing down since he was exhausted from the shocking brutality of what he'd witnessed. He wasn't used to running or brutality. He watched three of the officers lower her body from the makeshift cross. They were examining the KKK carved onto her chest.

"Those brutes!" one of the policemen exclaimed, lifting her slender form from the tree branches that covered her along with the shreds of her dress, and walked through the woods with a clumsy, wooden, almost-Frankenstein-like gait.

He had a teenage daughter. It was too much for him to bear. Things like this didn't happen in Mohegan, not lately anyway.

The other officers gathered bits of torn clothing and whatever evidence they could while Smith looked on, miffed. He was sorry he'd come back to the scene. He wasn't a Klan member, just in shock by the cruelty he'd seen. He put his head down, worried about his wife and children. Numbed by the turn of events, he walked up to one of the officers gathering shreds of Khadija's clothing and motioned that he wanted to say something.

The tall, lanky officer looked up at the thin man dressed in an expensive suit. "What is it?"

"I can tell you who did it if you'll guarantee me safety. No one must know I was here," mumbled Smith.

The other officers stopped in their tracks. One fumbled for a pair of handcuffs.

"Tell us. We'll provide witness protection." The officers took a deep breath in unison as he started to talk.

"It was the miners, you know, the Black ones," came out in a slurry mumble. Then he started to laugh at his own audacity.

The officers exchanged furious looks. They'd heard lies before. But this beat them all.

They cuffed him. "Tell us the truth. Those Black miners half scared to death of you Klansmen. And who killed Jameson?"

He struggled a bit with the handcuffs and his conscience; he knew he had to tell the truth.

"It was that Black girl, the whore from Maggie's house, the one who seduced Jameson. She killed him."

"You mean to tell us that slender slip of a girl killed Jameson with a rock? What was her motive? She's been brutally murdered and strung up on a makeshift cross. What's the meaning of all this? She was violated, beaten, almost martyrized. Who raped her?"

"Not me!" He squirmed and looked at the ground. "I never touched any woman but my wife in my life! I'm not going to fraternize with a she-devil. I'm not a Klansman. I have principles...and a wife!"

"But someone did. Spill! Spill the beans now, or we'll prosecute you for the cold-blooded rape and murder of a young Black girl!"

"Oh, no! My wife...she'd kill me! It was Jameson—" He stopped, muted by his own confession.

"The senator raped and murdered this girl?"

They were incredulous.

"He only raped her! She threw a rock at him, blinded him! Then he staggered, fell on that boulder, hit his head hard, and died, but he didn't kill her." He began to sweat profusely.

"So who did?"

They tightened his handcuffs, pushing him against a large boulder.

"The...It's hard to say. There were so many of them." He looked at the ground and shut up. He felt weak thinking of what might be in store for him.

The police stared at each other.

"You mean you all raped her and then killed her?"

They pushed his head back against the rock.

"Nah. Not me! I'm not that kind of—"

"That kind of Klansman? Just a sweet little mama's boy out having a night on the town?"

"Yeah..." He took a deep breath, raised his head high, and blurted, "I'm a scientist who works at Fort Bener."

The police stared at him in contempt.

One of them slapped his knee and started to laugh. "Now we know you're lying! No Klansman ever worked in a lab. You're not too innocent to tell the judge what you just told us. We've got witnesses. Now what's your name?"

"Jack Smith, supervisor of the CRE project at Fort Bener. You've got to give me anonymity. I came with Bill Jameson out of curiosity. I met him at Fort Bener. There are documents to prove it."

The officers exchanged looks. This was a strange duck.

"What're we gonna do with nut case?" asked one of the policemen, brushing mud from his shirt.

"We'll let the judge figure that out," said his partner, squinting his eyes as he gave Jack a good look.

He was clean-cut, hair cut close to his head with a longish face, the face of an intellectual. The officers led him through the underbrush toward a squad car with the hounds following, heads down, sniffing the ground.

Chapter 13

Walter was patting Ellie's hand in their bedroom when he heard their daughters walk upstairs, holding a breakfast tray with flowers in a tiny vase along with the scrambled eggs and bacon. Sojourner smiled hesitantly at her mother, always so capable and vivacious, lying in bed after spending a week in the hospital. Her sister followed, sitting next to Ellie. She took her hand in hers and patted it.

"You've been through an awful lot, Mom," she said, giving her a sympathetic look.

"It was a close call." Ellie sighed. "Svetlana and Khadija weren't so lucky." She moved to a sitting position so that she could eat from the tray. "I'm so happy to see my girls!" She squeezed their hands.

They hugged her gently, for she had just recovered from a serious concussion. The silver barrette had saved her life.

"I'm lucky to be with you. I wish poor Khadija and Svetlana could say the same."

They took a collective deep breath.

"They don't come much closer than that," said Morrow, "But my Ellie has got nine lives! Praise be!"

Ellie took a sip from the orange juice that was on the tray.

"A bullet never stopped a Morrow," she said.

"What are you girls planning to do while you're here?"

"We want to find Khadija's little sister and brother!" said Chrissy.

Ellie and Walter exchanged worried looks.

"Where do you plan on finding them?" asked Morrow, pushing a shock of white hair off his furrowed brow. He didn't like the sounds of this venture.

"Maybe at the Covenant House in DC," replied Chrissy. "I heard Khadija was giving them money for food and stuff since they were homeless. The Covenant House takes good care of the homeless." She smiled, hoping to convince her parents that they could help.

"Do you know their names? How're you gonna find them?" Ellie looked tired and a bit stricken. *Not everybody's got a silver barrette to see them through danger.* She was worried.

"Don't you worry, Mom." Sojourner wrapped her slender arms around her mother, cradling her, rocking her back and forth, hoping to soothe her worries.

Chrissy put her arm around her father's waist.

He turned and looked at her. "What do you want, sweet pie? You know your mother and I will worry if you go to DC looking for kids you don't even know." His brow furrowed as he thought of what could happen in Washington, D.C. to two young women.

"What are their names?" cooed Chrissy.

Sojourner took a deep breath. They had to know their names.

"Promise not to stay out past ten o'clock? The streets of Washington can get dangerous at night."

"We promise," chorused Sojourner and Chrissy.

"Harriet and Medgar."

"Harriet and Medgar? Like Medgar Evers?" Sojourner's eyes opened wide as she thought of the civil rights leader gunned down in his own driveway.

"The same," said Ellie in a quiet voice. She was worried about her girls. *What a world* she thought, feeling uneasy.

Chrissy and Soj jumped up and down, excited at the prospect of helping find Khadija's siblings who they knew needed help. They kissed their parents, bumped fists and ran to get in their car, an old Chevy.

Morrow and Ellie glanced at them and each other, not knowing what to think of their daughters' impetuous venture.

*****

Sojourner and Chrissy drove to the nation's capital in high spirits. Chrissy drove while Soj chattered away.

"We can find them and help them find whatever they need. These kids have got to be special. Their sister was."

Sojourner glanced at her. "We have to tell them that Khadija is dead," she said, suddenly somber.

"That too." Chrissy gave her sister a chastened look.

Maybe she was overdoing it. Maybe they wouldn't be able to find them. Soj shivered and let Chrissy drive in silence.

Chrissy drove along the winding West Virginia road fast, her dark eyes taking in the dense woods of broad-leaved trees, the deep-green foliage, as she stepped on the gas pedal, her slender foot encased in L. L. Bean boots that her parents had given her for Christmas. Her sister leaned back in the passenger seat, mumbling something about slowing down and school.

"Huh?"

Sojourner turned to Chrissy and yelled, "Ya like your classes this quarter?" She wished she'd slow down. *Chrissy always drives too fast* ran through her turgid mind. She knew finding Khadija's homeless siblings wasn't going to be easy.

"Environmental studies is way cool," Chrissy shot back, "but I'm starting to like my American history classes better." She shrugged her shoulder, nonchalant.

"I always hated history. All those dates and wars. It was boring. Pure memorization," said Soj.

"Yeah, I know, but Adrianne makes all those desiccated old Puritans come alive. She even quotes Cotton Mather, 'Dyed in the blood of the Lamb.' She wears flowing magenta capes and tons of rings. She's not like the others. She's dramatic!"

"Sounds religious." Soj laughed at the idea. "Like Sunday school." She leaned back in her seat, trying to ignore Chrissy's driving.

Chrissy shook her head. "Nope. She's real. She breathes life into those old Puritans. She's teaching us about Harriet Tubman and a couple of Quaker women who helped her run the Underground Railroad now. What about your classes?"

Soj twisted a strand of her long, thick dark hair into a nervous knot. "They're good." She wasn't used to Chrissy acting so headstrong. "How about Mom shooting that Russian spy?"

Chrissy jerked her head toward Soj, moving the steering wheel enough to make the car bank to the right.

Soj sat up fast.

"She saved Dad's life! And she survived a KKK bullet to the head. I'm proud of her."

"Yeah, me too, but her killin' that spy surprised me. Mom was never a marksman."

"He wasn't far away, and she knew how to shoot a rifle. There's so much more to Mom than we realize." She grinned at the thought. "Anyway, here we are, chasin' after two homeless kids in DC. Maybe we should have a gun."

Sojourner's smooth brow wrinkled into a frown. "Once somebody's got a gun, things happen."

"You mean they end up using it?" Chrissy pressed the gas pedal even harder, nearly sending the car off the winding road.

Soj started to feel a twinge of fear crawl down her spine. Her sister could be heedless.

"What do you think?" Soj shot Chrissy a dark look.

She was as worried about her driving as she was about packing a gun.

"Not sure," replied Chrissy, slowing a bit. "Just as soon not be packing one."

"Yeah." Soj nodded her head in agreement. "Guns are bad news."

Chrissy narrowed her eyes as she pressed the gas pedal harder and harder.

Soj took a deep breath. "Hey, aren't you going a bit fast, Stirling Moss?" She knew she had to do something, or they'd have an accident.

"Our mother almost got killed!" yelled Chrissy, flooring the gas pedal. "A beautiful Black girl was gang-raped and murdered... most cruelly." She took her foot off the pedal for a second, breathing deeply.

"You think I don't know?"

"Well, say something!" Chrissy tightened her hands on the steering wheel and jammed the gas pedal to the floor again.

"What can I say? This is straight out of the pages of Black history, Mississippi Burning, rape, torture. Those men weren't Puritans. That's for sure!"

The broad-leaved trees whizzed by them at a vertiginous speed. Chrissy started to sniffle.

Soj looked at her. "You're freaking out! Pull over!"

Chrissy jammed her foot on the gas pedal one last time, pushed the speedometer to ninety, started to sob, and pulled over with a lurch. Soj felt her body thrust forward and would've gone through the window if the seat belt hadn't been fastened so tight. The car came to an abrupt halt. Both girls stared blankly in front of themselves into the dark, quiet woods.

Soj put her arm around her sobbing sister. "Come on, Chrissy. We've got to make Mom and Dad proud of us. Quit crying. We can do this."

Chrissy put her head on Soj's shoulder. She felt reassured. Soj hugged her sister, helped her undo her seat belt, got out of the car, and walked around to where Chrissy sat, exhausted.

"I can drive," she intoned softly.

She didn't want to upset Chrissy, who was clearly unfit to drive. Chrissy looked up at her. "Okay. You drive."

They grinned at each other. Chrissy got out, and Soj slid into the driver's seat. Chrissy walked over to the passenger's side.

"What beautiful trees," she said absently.

She got in the car and buckled up, and the girls resumed their conversation as if nothing had happened. Soj was the levelheaded one, and they both had known that for years.

As they talked, the road darkened. Soon they saw lights and turned onto the Beltway that led to Washington, D.C. The granite statues of lions that guarded the bridge that crossed over the Potomac River to Washington appeared.

"I love Washington." Chrissy sighed.

"Me too. The Lincoln and Jefferson Memorials…the way they're lit up gold and sometimes pink makes it seem magical."

"It is magical," said Chrissy, feeling calm after her wild ride.

Sojourner drove down Pennsylvania Avenue past a homeless encampment. She saw a foot protrude from a blanket.

"Then again…"

"How can people let other people lie out in the freezing cold on the sidewalk?" said Chrissy, frowning. "Let's stop and try to help them!"

Soj stared at her excited sister. "We're on mission Harriet and Medgar. Don't have time for every homeless person in Washington. Come on!" She frowned at Chrissy.

"I know someone who lets them stay in her spare room." She grinned. "That's how it should be! People sharing what they got with other people!" Chrissy nearly shouted.

Soj slowed the car and looked at her exuberant, often over-wrought sister. "I agree, but you must admit…Who shares her place with the homeless?" She tossed her dark locks over her shoulder to glance at Chrissy.

"Oh, she's a little eccentric. People think she's bringing men in to sleep with. They say bad things about her." She shook her frizzy blond head. "She's just generous and open minded."

"I swear to my grandmammy! People always think the worst! I think they like to think that way 'cuz they aren't doing a thing…I just don't understand them."

"Well, the homeless must like her."

The girls looked at one another and started to laugh.

Then Chrissy started to pout. "Why are you always so…so mean to me?"

Soj turned a corner and headed toward the homeless shelter. "What are you talking about? We're sisters!"

Chrissy wiped a tear away. "Yeah, but you always take charge like I'm not capable or something."

Soj shot Chrissy an annoyed look. "Look, we've got to find these kids, maybe at the shelter or maybe in the streets. Who knows? We can't get distracted by our emotions. You know I love the homeless."

"But what about me?" A chastened Chrissy sniffed, rubbing her nose on her coat sleeve.

Soj turned an upset face to Chrissy. "You're my sister. We're close, almost like twins. I'd do anything for you. I love you. You know I do."

They exchanged wide-eyed looks filled with regret for what Chrissy had said.

"Sorry, Soj. I love you too. I'm just getting overly emotional. You know how I am."

Soj stared at the road ahead. "I sure do. Better believe it. I'd do anything for you."

"And I'd do anything for you, even if you do look like Meghan Markle."

Sojourner burst out laughing. "Stop it! I have long dark hair like her. Big deal!"

"And a glowing oval face—"

"That shines in the dark! That's why everyone uses me for a flashlight!" Soj smirked.

She laughed at her own joke just as a girl in ultra-high stilettos and a slit-to-the-thigh dress walked into an ultra-chic club.

"You're right, Chris. These snobby rich white folks can give a girl heartburn."

Chrissy turned to her sister and, in a quiet voice, asked, "Have they done it to you?"

Soj jerked her head toward her sister. Her jaw dropped.

"You mean the race thing?"

Chrissy turned to stare at her sister as a bleached-blond girl wearing a fancy dress crossed in front of them.

Soj stopped the car and waited for her to get to the sidewalk before saying anything. Chrissy beat her to it.

"I'm not dark complected, but I've got frizzy hair like Mom. Every now and then, someone makes a remark. Maybe that's what I get for going to Vassar instead of Howard." She put her head down, remembering a few of the frizzy-hair remarks. Not many, but one was enough. "I pretty much ignore them. Once, I told them I was proud of my nappy hair. Then they asked me what nappy hair was. Vassar is so white-bread…" She trailed off. "I got used to the insidious—"

"Implications," finished Soj, her brow furrowed as she remembered a few of the dark-skin comments she'd heard at her university. "Maybe we can help some kids who have darker skin and kinkier hair than we do, didn't have the advantage of having a senator for a father, a wonderful, inclusive father who married a woman who— Well, Mom's Black. We're lucky, you know." She winced as memories of hurtful remarks ran through her head.

A plain brick building loomed ahead with nothing to distinguish it other than the group of shabbily dressed kids waiting outside.

"That's the Covenant House!" Chrissy pointed at it, excited. "They must know something about Khadija's sister and brother."

"Let's hope so," said Soj as she parked in the only vacant space near the building, a renovated warehouse painted a warm shade of cream.

A security guard stood outside the double doors at the entrance.

The girls got out of their car, walked up to her, and asked her if they could speak to the person in charge. She gave them the once-over and pointed to a desk inside where a heavyset woman sat with her dark hair pulled back into a bun. She looked up from her paperwork as Soj walked toward her, hand extended. Chrissy followed, wishing she'd taken the lead.

"Good evening. I'm Sojourner Morrow, and this is my sister, Chrissy."

The amiable-looking plump woman wearing an old pair of blue jeans and a parka that had seen better days smiled. "How can I help you, ladies?"

She hoped they didn't need a bed because the Covenant House was full and then some. They wore nice, shiny parkas and skinny jeans with no rips, but you never could tell. She'd seen all kinds of people. Some walked in dressed to the nines, newly evicted from their homes, with two or three children. It was the children she could give a bed to. The Covenant House helped underage children, not adults, and these girls looked like they were over eighteen.

"We're looking for Harriet and Medgar, Khadija's younger sister and brother. I think her legal name was Tina Jameson."

The woman breathed a sigh of relief. "I'm Marion. I haven't seen them for a few days. They go to Maggie's pretty often to see their sister. She makes pretty good money there and helps feed them."

Chrissy and Sojourner exchanged grim looks.

Soj nudged Chrissy, who blurted out, "She's...she's no longer with us."

Marion's eyes widened. "What do you mean?"

Grisly scenarios flashed through her mind. She knew Maggie took care of her girls, but who knew what happened when they left?

"She was killed by a group of vicious men," said Soj, staring her in the eye. "We think her brother and sister would like to attend her funeral."

"Not Khadija! You mean Tina Jameson is dead? She was so nice...so generous!" She drew in a deep breath, averting her face. This was too shocking even for her. "She was doing good at Maggie's!" She frowned. "Forget that I said that!"

"Could you tell us where Maggie's is? We want to help her little brother and sister." Soj looked down, not wanting to face the woman's shock. It was so awful.

Marion inhaled deeply.

A girl wearing ripped jeans with Love tattooed just below her scalp on her forehead ran by. "It's the whorehouse in Georgetown. They turned me down 'cuz of my tattoo."

Soj grabbed her by the arm. She struggled to free herself.

"Sorry!" said Soj. "Could you take us there? We've got to find her younger brother and sister. We want to help them."

The girl with the forehead tattoo stared at them. "I need help just as bad as they do!"

"We'll try to help you too," blurted Chrissy, shaking her blond head, her smile bright like a beacon in the dim lights.

"Are you one of us?"

Soj stepped in front of Chrissy, facing the girl. "We're octoroons," she said, lifting her head proudly.

"Yeah. You're not Black, but you got dark eyes, and your skin isn't lily white, and your sister has kinky hair. That's enough. Let's go.

You got a car? It's in Georgetown." She tugged at her crop top, which showed her navel ring.

"Yes! Please take us there! We'll make it worth your while," said Chrissy, rubbing her fingers together.

"How much is it worth to you?"

The girl stood back, examining them. She knew anyone who didn't wear thrift-store clothes couldn't be trusted and might have money.

"Fifty dollars," said Chrissy.

Soj gave her a dirty look. "We're just asking a favor. If you need money, you don't have to get it from us that way. We want to help you."

"You crazy," said the girl. "Okay. Let's go!"

Marion shook her head in dismay as they piled into Soj and Chrissy's Chevy. She hoped it would turn out all right.

They sped away toward Georgetown, talking a mile a minute. Soj drove faster than usual.

*****

The large man at the door of Maggie's raised a quizzical eyebrow as the three girls tumbled out of their car. They didn't look like customers, but all kinds of people came to Maggie's. He fingered the Glock in his vest just in case.

You never know, he thought. *All kind of people come here.*

"What you girls doing here?" he asked in a stern voice. Then he recognized the girl with the tattoo on her forehead. "You know Maggie doesn't want to see you."

Soj stepped up and said, "We're looking for Khadija's kid sister and brother. We want to help them."

"Oh, little White saviors." He said, his voice laced with sarcasm as he looked them up and down. *Those two too gentrified for this place.* "Are you here for business or pleasure?" He laughed at his own sally.

Chrissy stepped up in front of him, craning her neck because he was at least six feet, five inches tall. Maggie knew how to pick her guards.

"Could we speak to the manager?" she asked as politely as the sweet Vassar girl she was imitating.

"Business or pleasure? You haven't answered my question."

Soj nudged Chrissy, taking her place in front of the implacable doorman.

"Neither. We're looking for Khadija's brother and sister. We want to help them." She gave him her best no-nonsense look.

"Yeah, yeah. Okay. Go on in. Maggie's sitting at the table with a couple of the girls." He grunted and moved aside, opening the door for them.

When the girl with the tattoo on her forehead passed by, he stuck his arm out. "Not you. Maggie already said you didn't make the grade."

Soj turned around. "Make the grade? Seriously?"

Her blood started to boil. It made her mad to think a girl had to meet a certain standard to be a prostitute.

She grabbed Marion by the arm. "She's coming with us."

Chrissy marched into the front room of Maggie's and saw her. You couldn't miss her because she was so much older than the teens sitting around in expensive, provocative apparel. One wore only a bustier and skin-tight pants that were almost transparent. You could see everything. And she looked like she was only about fourteen-years-old. She was serving drinks to the older men dressed in expensive suits or hangout clothes. Some sported diamond cuff links.

Ugh, she thought.

Maggie stood, brushed the cake crumbs off her revealing red velvet low-cut dress, and walked up to them. She saw the LOVE-tattooed girl and gave the men a sly wink. The other two looked like librarians to her.

"What can I do for you, young ladies?"

"We're trying to find Khadija's brother and sister," said Chrissy, looking hopeful.

All of a sudden, a young boy started playing the piano and singing a Fats Domino song. He was all of twelve years old if that.

"Khadija's on leave. Maybe permanent leave. She hasn't been around for a few days," said Maggie, narrowing her eyes to piercing slits, hoping these weren't social workers. What a pain in the butt they could be.

"She's on permanent leave," said Soj.

"How do you know?"

"She was raped and murdered by a bunch of KKK brutes. We want to help her siblings. My mom and dad are making sure she gets a proper funeral."

Maggie took a deep breath. "Let's sit over here," she said, motioning to an empty table, "and have some drinks."

The four women sat down and eyed each other.

"How did you know?" asked Maggie.

"Some men targeted her, Dr. Svetlana Jameson, and my mother after Mom announced she was running for senator of West Virginia. Mom was saved by a silver barrette in her hair."

Maggie's eyes widened. "That was pretty damn lucky." She took a swig of her cranberry vodka.

"It was a miracle!" said Chrissy, wiggling around in her chair. "Now she's running for senator of West Virginia!"

"It'll take a miracle to get her elected," said Maggie, gulping some more cranberry vodka down. "Women have a tough time getting elec—"

"Times are changing, Maggie," interrupted Sojourner.

"Yeah, the more they change, the more they stay the same." Maggie was cynical to the bone. She'd seen too many smart women's lives ruined.

The fourteen-year-old girl dressed in the filmy but expensive Dior walked over to them. "Can I get you ladies something to drink?" Her voice was sweet and polite.

Maggie had given her a free dinner.

"I'll have a gin and tonic," said the Love-tattooed girl.

"Ginger ale, please," said Chrissy. She smiled a sweet little smile. "Is that all?"

"Isn't that enough?" Sojourner pushed a lock of her dark hair out of her face and smiled at the Love girl.

The girl smiled back, impressed by the beauty of this girl whose skin glowed like burnished alabaster.

"What's your name?"

"Oh, I don't really...I mean, I'm Khadija's little sister." She smiled at them, proud of being the sister of a working woman who helped her and her brother survive.

"Khadija?" chorused Chrissy and Sojourner.

A youngster started banging on Maggie's piano, trying to imitate Fats Domino, singing, "I'm walking. Yes, indeed, I'm walking..."

He was small for his age with a ready smile and dimples in his chubby cheeks.

"That's my brother." Khadija's sister laughed. "We're waiting for her to come get us. Maggie's been really nice..."

The chandelier overhead seemed to spin, its bright lights shimmering in the dark room.

Sojourner grabbed Chrissy's hand and turned her head to face Maggie. "Don't they know?"

"Know what?" said Maggie, adjusting her low-cut bodice.

"Khadija's dead," Sojourner whispered to the young girl, trying to use a soft voice to break the news; but it didn't work.

The little girl shook her head violently. "No, no! Stop lying to me! My sister is coming to get us!"

Maggie put her hand on the young girl's arm. "Not tonight, honey, not tonight."

"When is she coming?" demanded the girl.

"Not ever," said the LOVE-tattooed girl.

She swiveled around in her chair to avoid Khadija's little sister's face.

Maggie stood up and hustled her over to a sofa. She took her in her velvet-covered arms and hugged her. "Honey, Khadija's gone. They want to help you. They'd like to know if you want to go to her funeral."

Khadija's sister, Harriet, had dissolved into a puddle of tears. Her brother was still banging "I'm Walking" on the piano.

Chapter 14

It was a bright, sunny day, with a bit of a breeze unfurling some of the ladies' upswept hair in a large audience in front of the Charlestown, West Virginia, capitol building. The sun shone brightly on a woman's eagle-shaped barrette in her kinky blond hair. Ellie Morrow stood erect and proud with Walter Morrow standing off to one side. She smiled at the crowd. They let out a big cheer. Her smile turned into a huge grin. She was thrilled at her prospects.

"If you elect me to represent you in Congress, I'll do just that!"

They cheered even louder.

"I've watched my husband fight for workers' rights, civil rights, and women's rights! I plan to do the same. I plan to fight for every citizen's rights and justice for all with my God-given heart and soul!'

The crowd jumped to its feet. "Huzzah!" they shouted so loud that Ellie could barely hear herself think, but she continued with her speech.

"There's been some wrongs done in the beautiful state of West Virginia that I intend to right! The coal miners always get the shaft."

The crowd roared.

"And some unscrupulous people have taken advantage of people who couldn't defend themselves. I'm going to defend you!" She took off her barrette so that they could see it. "This silver eagle, the symbol of our union with the United States of America, saved my life just a few weeks ago!"

The crowd went crazy with patriotic fervor. Charles, Adelaide's husband, stood in front with their two children.

"We chose not to fight with the Confederacy in 1861. We chose not to be a slave state. We chose freedom over oppression, right over wrong!".

The crowd started to chant, "Ellie, Ellie, Ellie…"

"My dear husband, Walter Morrow, stood by your side just as I'll stand by your side, only this time I have a personal wrong to right."

Ellie motioned for Charles to stand next to her on the stage. He mounted the steps to the stage and walked over to where she stood, a bit stooped but unwavering. He held his two children by the hand. They blinked, unused to so much attention, but they didn't cry. Khadija's sister and brother, dressed in new clothes Ellie had bought them for the occasion, mounted the stage and stood next to her, bowing their heads to honor Khadija. They had never stood in front of a crowd of people before and felt shy in addition to the heavy blanket of mourning that had enveloped them.

"These children lost their beloved sister when some cowardly men covering their shame with sheets drove me, Dr. Svetlana Jameson, and Khadija off the road. They shot both me and Dr. Jameson. I was saved by this here silver eagle, but dear Dr. Jameson and our beloved Khadija weren't as lucky. They were killed by the Klansmen, one of whom has revealed the identities of most of the others due to the swift diligence of our Mohegan police force!"

Walter Morrow applauded from where he stood while the crowd went wild.

"Justice, justice, justice!" they roared.

"There will be justice! These men will be tried, and they won't be let off the hook because of the color of their skin or whatever high office they occupied! They are guilty as sin! I, for one, recognized their voices, and we have the sworn testimony of one of them who participated in the brutal murder of two innocent women!"

The crowd surged forward. "Trial, trial. Hang them. Justice now!" They were delirious.

Ellie put out her hand, palm forward, to calm the crowd.

"In all due respect, we will give you justice, and we have already buried Khadija, a descendant of the slaves who worked on the Jameson plantation, in a hidden graveyard where slaves buried their own before the war. Her sister and brother wanted it that way."

Everyone knew she meant the Civil War; it was the unending war they still fought in their hearts.

"If elected, I intend to make this graveyard a memorial to those who suffered the gross injustice of being owned by another human being. I will also fight for higher wages for miners and the working class, for better working conditions down in the mining shafts, and better working conditions and equal rights for all workers. And better pay!"

The crowd surged toward Ellie, the Foleys and Khadija's siblings—surrounding them with roses and embracing them, finally hoisting Ellie onto two sturdy men's shoulders, one Black and one white. Then two miners walked over to Walter and hoisted him high on their shoulders, pushing their way through the crowd so he could be next to his wife. She stretched out her hands and took his into hers. The jubilant crowd couldn't stop cheering, and Ellie couldn't stop tears from rolling down her face.

She knew she could beat her opponent, another flashy hypocrite, and ensure these good people their god given rights.

Walter cheered after the crowd deposited him in front of the meeting hall, hand in hand with Ellie. His shock of white hair blew off his brow as he announced, "Ellie Morrow will bring justice to West Virginia, justice for all!" He shouted loud and clear. "And I'm throwing my hat in the ring to run for president of the United States of America!"

The crowd went wild, thrilled by Walter's announcement. They cheered until they were hoarse.

Ellie stepped forward, put her arms in the air, and declared, "Justice for all, Black, white, mixed-blood, Brown, all workers, and all people!"

The cheering continued, unabated until Ellie and Walter ducked into her Tesla and drove away, waving out the car windows.

The ghosts in the hidden slave graveyard jostled one another slightly to stand vigil over their new arrival, their heads bent in prayer.

Svetlana's fifteen-year-old daughter wept over her mother's casket in Moscow. She vowed to find out who killed her father and to honor her parents.

Other titles by the author:

Never Marry in Morocco, The Bushy Daughters Go to War and Find Rumi, Touch Me, Touch Me Not and Rich White Americans.

About the Author

Ms. Dale is a firm advocate that, with a strong will and moral courage, right will triumph over wrong. Her main inspiration is Abraham Lincoln who, "with malice toward none and charity for all," saw the United States through its most trying times, the Civil War of 1861–1865. She hopes that *Tumpery* will shed light on that which hardens the heart and that which heals the soul.